#9 BRING ME A DREAM

#9 BRING ME A DREAM

ROBERT JAMES

Based upon the television series "Eerie Indiana" created by Karl Schaefer and José Rivera

AN AVON CAMELOT BOOK

This is a work of fiction. Names, characters, places, and incidents either are the product of the author's imagination or are used fictitiously. Any resemblance to actual events, locales, organizations, or persons, living or dead, is entirely coincidental and beyond the intent of either the author or the publisher.

AVON BOOKS
A division of
The Hearst Corporation
1350 Avenue of the Americas
New York, New York 10019

Copyright © 1998 by Hearst Entertainment, Inc.
Based on the Hearst Entertainment television series entitled "Eerie Indiana" created by Karl Schaefer and José Rivera
Published by arrangement with Hearst Entertainment, Inc.
Excerpt from *Eerie Indiana #10: Finger-Lickin' Strange* copyright © 1998 by Hearst Entertainment, Inc.
Visit our website at **http://www.AvonBooks.com**
Library of Congress Catalog Card Number: 97-94947
ISBN: 0-380-79785-2

First Avon Camelot Printing: April 1998

CAMELOT TRADEMARK REG. U.S. PAT. OFF. AND IN OTHER COUNTRIES, MARCA REGISTRADA, HECHO EN U.S.A.

Printed in the U.S.A.

OPM   10 9 8 7 6 5 4 3 2 1

#9 BRING ME A DREAM

PROLOGUE
PROLOGUE

*M*y name is Marshall Teller. Not too long ago, I lived in New Jersey, just across the river from New York City. It was crowded, polluted, and full of crime. I loved it. But my parents decided to find a better life for my sister and me. So we moved to a place so wholesome, so squeaky clean, so ordinary that you could only find it on TV—Eerie, Indiana.

It's the American Dream come true, right? Wrong. Sure, my new hometown looks normal enough. But look again. It's the hall of fame of weirdness. Item: Elvis lives on my paper route. Item: Bigfoot eats out of my trash. Item: I see unexplained flashing lights in the sky once a week.

Since I moved here, I've been stalked by a tornado, delivered a letter for a ghost, and lived the same day over and over because of a cursed snow globe. Every time something bizarre happens, I think life just can't get any weirder. Then I turn the corner and find something even stranger waiting to shake my hand. But no matter how weird Eerie gets, nobody seems to notice.

Nobody except my friend Simon Holmes. Simon is my next-door neighbor. He's lived in Eerie his whole life, and he's the only other person who knows just how freaky this place is. Together, we've been keeping a record of all the stuff that happens around here. We've faced some of Eerie's strangest inhabitants and lived to tell about it, from the talking dogs that tried to take over the town to the guys who arrest anyone who hasn't kept up with daylight savings time. I told you this place was weird.

Don't believe me? You will.

1

*T*here aren't too many places where you can get into trouble by going to sleep.

Unfortunately Eerie, Indiana, is one of them.

But let me start at the beginning.

Breaking in a new breakfast cereal is tough enough, but trying to choose between oven-fried rice pork balls and cocoa-flavored beef corn chips at eight o'clock in the morning on the first day of summer vacation is close to impossible. My mom didn't see the dilemma. She had gotten these two cereals the day before because the store was out of my favorite, plain old Cheerios. And now she wanted to inflict one or the other on me. My choice.

"Come on, now, Marshall, which one will it be?" she asked, pointing at the boxes. "Pork balls or beef corn? Or should I make you a bowl of both?"

"I don't know, Mom. Neither one sounds very good."

"Mr. Radford at World of Stuff said they're the latest thing."

I rolled my eyes. Mr. Radford owns World of Stuff, which is probably the world's best convenience store. You can get just about anything there, from sneakers to rocket engines.

But not Cheerios. And not decent cereal, either. Mr. Radford's a nice guy, but he has an Eerie perspective on things. Those cereals are probably really hot—but only in Eerie, not the real world.

"The boxes say they're very nutritious." My mom took a handful of each cereal. "Want to try them dry first?"

"I don't think so."

"Since when are you a fussy eater?" she asked. The corners of her mouth folded down into a mom-frown. That's the look mothers get when you do something they don't understand. My mom uses that frown on me so much I think there's a permanent hinge in her mouth.

"Can't I have a piece of toast or an egg or something?"

"These cereals are more nutritious," said my mom, tossing a few bites of each into her mouth. "The box says that they contain an entire medicine cabinet's worth of vitamins in one bite. And they're very tast—"

She meant to say *tasty,* but she didn't finish. Instead, she ran from the room gagging. When she came back

4

a few minutes later she announced that we'd all have eggs and toast for breakfast.

By then my sister, Syndi, and my dad had come down to the kitchen. Dad brought his copy of the *Eerie Examiner* to read with his coffee. The sports section was the first thing he flipped to. Since we were from New Jersey, he liked to follow the teams from back East. But it could be frustrating.

"Looks like the baseball game ended after the paper's deadline again," said my dad. "There's only a partial score. Yankees three."

"How many runs did the other team have?" I asked.

"Doesn't say," answered my father. "It's only a partial score."

He looked through the paper, browsing in the classified ads. "Well look at this," he said. "A 'sixty-five Mustang convertible for sale. Red. Three speed. V-8. Boy, I'd love to have one of those."

"Dream on, dear," said my mom.

"I will. Tonight," promised my dad.

Syndi had brought her driver's license manual to the table to study. She flipped through it, looking for important facts to memorize.

"Now here's something I didn't know," she announced. " 'Before making a turn the driver must signal his intention.' That means you have to turn on the signal before you turn.''

"Duh," I said.

"Come on, honey, you know you have to use the blinker when you make a turn," said my dad.

"You never do," Syndi pointed out.

My father went back to reading the paper.

"I don't think this section is for me," added my sister. "The book says *he,* and I'm not a he. Not that I wouldn't mind finding a nice dreamboat to drive around with."

When Syndi first announced that she was going to take the driver's test, my feeling was, go for it. After all, it might be pretty useful to have someone around to drive me places I wanted to go—namely, out of Eerie. But that was before I saw her behind the wheel. Now I put my football helmet on any time she asks for a practice drive.

Mom was just setting out the first batch of scrambled eggs when what looked like a small rocket fired off the counter. It pounded into the ceiling and rebounded to the floor in flames.

Actually, it wasn't a rocket at all. It was just the toast.

"It's really time to get a new toaster," my mom said, retrieving a piece from the other side of the room. She plopped the mangled slice on my dad's plate, hoping he would take a hint.

"Here's an idea," suggested my dad as he brushed off the burn marks. "Why don't we take back the gift Uncle Fred gave us and exchange it for a toaster?"

"You know we can't do that. I promised him I would send it back so he could find something else for us."

"Tell him to get us a toaster, then."

"He said he already has something in mind."

"Great," said my father. He was being sarcastic. It was just like me saying I'd just "love" to take out the garbage.

Uncle Fred's gift was sitting on the counter. It was a clock.

Kind of. It was really a statue of a guy in shepherd's clothes, holding his hands over his eyes. His stomach was a big round clock. No matter how you adjusted it, the hands only told the correct time for Warsaw, Poland.

Warsaw was where my Uncle Fred was living this month. He works for the same company as my dad: Things, Inc. They have different jobs, though. My father checks stuff out. He's always getting new things to try, like petroleum-based banana flavoring. One drop of that in your water supply and you'll be brushing your teeth with banana splits for the rest of your life. Dad's job is why we live in Eerie—statistically speaking, it's the most normal place in America.

Statistics don't just lie, they laugh at you.

Anyway, my uncle's job is different. He travels the world looking for stuff to test. He likes to send Mom and Dad a gift every so often, usually to celebrate some holiday like National Seat Belt Day or Love Your Dictionary Week. In this case, it had been Polish Clock Day.

I used to call my Uncle Fred "Weird Uncle Fred," until I moved to Eerie and found out what world-class weirdness was really like.

"That reminds me," said my mother, looking at the clock. "I need someone to arrange for Uncle Fred's present to be picked up and delivered back to him. I have to be at the town council meeting at eight-forty-five."

"I can't do it," said Syndi. "I have my crash course today on the driver's test."

Crash course—her words.

"I'd love to do it," said my dad. "But I'm late for work."

Which, of course, left me. It sounds like an easy chore, right? Put the present back in its box, get out the phone book, make the call.

That was how my mom explained it, anyway.

"Use UPS or Federal Express or something like that," she said, putting on her lipstick as she ran out the door. "And don't forget to brush your teeth before you leave the house!"

I finished breakfast and got the box ready. The statue was about three feet tall. But since it was made out of plastic, it wasn't all that heavy. Once I had everything all taped up, I went to the phone book. All of the major delivery companies had toll-free numbers to arrange pickups. Not knowing any better, I started dialing.

Here's something that's not too surprising—neither UPS nor Federal Express will pick up or deliver to Eerie, Indiana.

The clerks on the phone were very polite at first. Then I told them where I was calling from. They all slammed the phone down so hard my ear rang. I was just about to give up when I saw an ad for a company called Dream Deliveries. The advertisement showed a van driving on a cloud. The words beneath the van said: YOU DREAM IT, WE'LL DELIVER IT. BEST RATES IN EERIE. CALL NOW, TOLL FREE.

Pretty good slogan, I thought. Of course, since no one else delivered in Eerie, they could charge a million dollars and still be the cheapest.

The lady on the other end answered the phone with a sleepy voice.

"Hello?"

"My name is Marshall Teller," I said. "And I wanted to know—do you stop in Eerie?"

"Of course we do, hon. What's your address?"

Right around then, the front doorbell rang. I figured it was my buddy Simon, so I didn't run and answer it or anything. But it did distract me a little. After I told the woman our address, the bell rang again.

"Good-bye now," said the woman.

"But I didn't tell you what to pick up!" I shouted into the phone.

It was too late. She had already hung up. Before I could punch the numbers again, a small man in a commando outfit burst into the room. He flashed a laser beam in my eyes, blinding me.

"Hey, Marshall. What are you doing?" croaked the commando.

Simon.

I put down the phone and shielded my eyes. "What's with that light?" I demanded.

"Isn't it cool? I got it at World of Stuff. It's a Special Forces Halogen Laser Flash Illumination Lantern, complete with aiming scope and pistol grip. What do you think?"

"I think you just blinded me."

"Great." Simon slid into a seat at the table and began

munching on some beef corn chips. "These are pretty good," he said. Then he got up to get a bowl and milk. "How come you didn't answer the doorbell? I had to pick the lock with my survivor scout knife."

"It wasn't locked."

"No wonder it took so long."

Simon is my best friend in Eerie, and the only normal kid I've found here. Still, even *he* can act strangely sometimes.

"So? You ready for the Gambino house?"

The Gambino house—also known as Eerie haunted house number twenty-six. We didn't know too much about it yet, except that it had been empty since the 1920s. We figured that meant it had been haunted at least that long, though you never can tell in Eerie.

Simon and I had big plans for our summer vacation. We wanted to make an inventory of all the haunted houses in town. Thanks to the card catalog at the library, plus some tips from people around town, we had a map of places to explore. We hoped by the end of the vacation we would have a shoe box full of ghost pictures. Heck, we might even get an interview with a ghost. Then we would have proof that Eerie is the center of weirdness for the entire planet.

While Simon ate his chips, I kept trying to call the delivery service back. It was always busy.

"Are we going ghost hunting or what?" demanded Simon when he finished the bowl.

"I have to make this call for my mom," I told him. "I'm having my Uncle Fred's present picked up."

"That neat shepherd clock?"

"One and the same."

"Do you think you could send them over to the junior high?" Simon asked. "I forgot to take my science project home on the last day of class."

"What do you want it for?"

"I'm afraid the ants will die if they're locked in the display case all summer. They don't have that much food."

Simon's science project was a giant ant farm made out of glass. The farm itself was pretty big, but what was giant about the project was the ants. Each one was about the size of a gerbil.

It's kind of a long story.

"I don't think I would trust a delivery service with giant ants," I told him. "You better get it yourself."

"Rats," said Simon. "Going to school is about the last thing I want to do today."

"They can wait a few days."

"I guess."

No matter how many times I tried, the phone line at Dream Deliveries was busy. Simon went into the living room and clicked on the TV. The local station was having a *Lost in Space* and *Lassie* marathon. Any other television channel would play one episode of *Lost in Space,* then one of *Lassie.* But not an Eerie station. They played both at the same time. Every time little Timmy got lost, a space alien would rescue him. Then Lassie would bite the alien, and Mrs. Robinson would serve everyone cake.

After I had been trying the phone number for twenty minutes, I decided I had enough. The lady had taken the address. That probably meant all I had to do was leave the package on the front step. And if not—well, I didn't think it was going to be a federal case if Uncle Fred's present didn't get picked up today. Even if I didn't know how much it would cost, I figured we couldn't do any better. No one but them would pick up in Eerie.

Besides, if I waited around much longer, Simon was going to get hooked on the TV shows. We'd spend hours watching TV—not a very good way to spend your first day of summer vacation.

Then again, maybe it would have been better than what happened next.

2

*O*ne thing I've always wondered about haunted houses—how come the front doors are never locked? Is it because ghosts want to be bothered? Or is it some unknown law of nature, like the fact that your shoelace will break only when you're late for school?

For whatever reason, the front door to the Gambino house swung wide open as soon as I reached for it. It squeaked and squealed on its hinges. The sound seemed to beckon us inside.

Or dare us to retreat.

We peered in from the porch. Simon turned on his commando light. The beam cut through the cobwebs of the hallway ahead. Dust filtered through the darkness. A dozen spiders scurried for the corners.

Serious ghost-hunting territory. Things were looking good.

I swung my Polaroid camera up and took a shot of the hallway, just to make sure it was working. I had loaded it up with special "Ghost-Plus" film, good in darkness or light. The film was World War II surplus and sold only at World of Stuff (two rolls and a bag of Fig Newtons for five dollars).

The picture filled in quickly. Plenty of shadows, but no ghosts. At least I knew the camera was working. I turned on my flashlight, and took a step across the threshold.

The floorboards groaned. Another good sign.

Even with Simon's heavy-duty light, the hallway was on the dark side. I took another step, then another, before I could make out what was ahead.

The front hallway extended back for maybe forty or fifty feet. There was a solid wall on my left. The beam from Simon's light shone on a row of old paintings. They looked to be outdoor scenes—people dancing around grape arbors and fires, stuff like that. Not too much haunting potential there.

Much more promising were the open doorways along the right side of the hallway. From where I was standing, I could see into about half of the first room. There was a fireplace and some furniture covered with sheets.

"You take the first room," I told Simon. "I'll go ahead to the next one."

Simon gripped his commando lantern tightly. I watched him step inside the room and begin sweeping the light around the corners. Then I walked ahead to the next room.

My flashlight caught something suspicious on the far wall inside. It looked like the shadowy outline of a body.

I nearly hiccuped with fright as it moved. It seemed to be coming toward me. For a second, I was paralyzed with fear.

Then I recovered. This is what I've been waiting for, I told myself. Real proof of a ghost. Real proof that Eerie, Indiana, is the center of weirdness.

I steadied my flashlight on the wall, then carefully reached for my camera. *No sudden movements,* I told myself. Don't do anything to spook the spook.

My finger was edging toward the camera button when I heard Simon squeal in surprise. I turned toward his shout, spinning my flashlight to the right.

Out of the corner of my eye, I saw the ghost move, too.

It wasn't a ghost at all. It was just my shadow. The two rooms were connected by an open archway. Simon's light had made me cast a shadow.

"I thought you were a ghost," said Simon, coming toward me.

"I thought I was, too. See anything suspicious?"

"Just you."

"All right. Let's go back out into the hallway and search the other rooms."

The false alarm made me even more cautious. I paused at the doorway, scanning the hallway. There were more open rooms along the right side. At the very end of the left side of the hallway was a single, closed doorway.

I was just thinking how odd it was to have only one door on that side of the house when something whacked me from behind. I fell over in a tumble, crashing straight into the wall.

And right through it.

"Sorry! Sorry!" shouted Simon. I couldn't see him. In fact, I couldn't see anything. I was lost in a cloud of dust.

"Are you okay, Marshall? Answer me! Mars?"

"I'm all right." I coughed. "The wall was made out of cardboard. My backpack broke my fall. What happened?"

"I thought I heard something move in the room behind us," he said. "I didn't mean to knock you over."

"Wow," I said as my eyes adjusted to the light. There were windows along the far side of the room. Dim light filtered through the dirty glass. It wasn't all that bright, but I could see. "Simon, I think this is a secret room or something."

"Or something," for sure. The room was huge. And moldy. Card tables, chairs, a roulette wheel, and what looked like a giant bar were all covered with about a foot of dust. All around the top was a balcony. The fancy railing was carved out of wood.

"It looks like an old club or something," I told Simon. "Come in with your light."

He came inside, flashing the laser all around. There was about a ton of cobwebs, but no ghosts.

If you spend any time at all in Eerie, you quickly become an expert on cobwebs. They come in a number of varieties. There are your round cobwebs, which basically look like the circles on a dart board. There are your triangular cobwebs, which look like the angles you measure in geometry class. And then there are the cock-eyed cobwebs, which are so weird the spider must have breathed laughing gas when he made them. They tangle and form shapes more complicated than a kaleidoscope.

The ones in here were mostly the last kind. Typical for Eerie.

"Looks like we found what we were looking for," announced Simon. "Let's go home."

"Go home? We haven't seen any ghosts yet."

"I told you, I heard something in the room back there."

18

"If there are going to be ghosts anywhere," I said, "they're going to be here. Ghosts love hidden rooms."

Simon sighed. He pointed his laser light around as I took photographs. More cobwebs, more dust, but nothing even remotely ghostly.

In Eerie, you have to consider that suspicious.

"This laser light is pretty good at showing dust," said Simon. "But maybe it's scaring the ghosts away."

"The ghosts are here, Simon. We just can't see them, that's all.

"What we need are eyeglasses that can make ghosts visible."

"That'd be pretty cool," I agreed. "But until we get some, we'll have to look for ghosts the way everybody else does. Here, take the baby powder from my backpack and spread it on the floor. Then check for footprints while I explore a little."

"I always get the boring jobs," Simon whined.

"It won't be boring if you see footprints."

I took a step toward the roulette wheel. In case you've never seen one, a roulette wheel has thirty-eight little black and red slots around the center spoke. Each slot has a number on it. You spin the wheel, and a small ball circles around and lands in one of the slots.

When we lived in New Jersey, we had a big party for my grandfather's eightieth birthday. The theme was

19

a casino. Syndi and I played the game for about three hours. We won about two hundred fake dollars. That was the last day I had any real luck.

"I wonder if the ghosts gamble here," I said, giving the wheel a good spin.

Dust flew all over the place. The ball shot around and around before landing in slot number thirteen.

I picked up the ball and gave the wheel another spin. Then I dropped the ball while the wheel was still turning. Again it landed in thirteen.

I told Simon to give the wheel a spin. He did, and the same thing happened.

Thirteen every time.

"Must be rigged," I said, giving it another spin just to see.

"Wha—What was that?" blurted Simon.

"What?"

"Didn't you hear that noise? It came from up there."

I whirled around and looked in the direction Simon was pointing. At the far end of the upstairs balcony there was a glass door. It had some words on it. The light was too dim and we were too far away to see what they might be.

"Think there's a ghost behind the door?" Simon asked. His voice was a little scared. Simon's still a little kid, so he gets spooked sometimes. Me, I like to save being spooked for something *really* scary. Like one of Mom's grapefruit-carrot cake recipes.

"I'm going up to check it out," I told him. "You stay here."

"No way."

"All right. But keep that light on. We're on full ghost alert."

"Gotcha."

The balcony stairs creaked a little as we walked up them. They seemed to say, "Turn back, turn back." Actually, it sounded more like, "The turtles are back, the turtles are back." But that didn't make sense.

The balcony was about twelve feet wide. A row of tables and chairs lined the far wall. We examined them carefully with Simon's light, but saw nothing suspicious. Slowly we made our way toward the door.

"Naughty Nannies," said Simon, reading the words on the door. "What do you think that means?"

I shrugged. This was one door that was locked. The keyhole was shaped like a warped *X*. None of the skeleton keys we'd brought with us worked.

"Think we should break the glass?" asked Simon. "Then you could stick your hand through and open it."

"My hand?"

"I'm not doing it."

I decided to explore more before breaking anything.

You can get in trouble for damaging someone's property—especially if that someone is a ghost.

"We can always do it later, if we can't find another way in," I told Simon. "We haven't finished looking around downstairs yet. I'd like to see if that roulette wheel is rigged, for starters."

"Check."

Simon led the way back down. I was beginning to get a bad feeling about haunted house number twenty-six. Sure, there was a "Trespass at your own risk of heart attack" sign on the lawn. And near the curb, a traffic sign warned drivers to be ready to brake for ghosts. But otherwise, there was nothing special about the outside: worn siding, broken windows, a couple of vultures hanging out on the roof. It could be any home in Eerie. Maybe it wasn't haunted after all.

We walked over to the roulette wheel. I gave it another spin, then got down to look for a magnet or something. Suddenly, I heard Simon say, "Hey, what do you think this button does?"

Before I could say anything, the floor disappeared below my feet. I felt myself plunging downward into a dark abyss. The last thing I remember thinking was, *Doesn't anybody in Eerie believe in plain old stairs?*

Then I blacked out.

3

I'm not sure how long I was unconscious. It probably wasn't very long, but in Eerie, an hour can be an hour or a minute. Sometimes it's a whole day. It's confusing, but it's Eerie.

While I was knocked out, I had a couple of weird dreams. In one of them, I was being chased through a maze of bathroom displays in a hardware store by a giant toothbrush. That might have been my brain's way of reminding me that I hadn't brushed my teeth after breakfast, even though Mom told me to.

The other dream I had didn't seem quite as weird— at least, not at the time. In that dream Simon and I had eyeglasses that let us see ghosts. The dream must have come from Simon's suggestion.

The glasses worked pretty well. I saw a headless horseman and a kid who could take his head off and kick it around like a soccer ball.

The dream ended before I saw anything really gruesome, though.

When I came to I realized I had fallen through some sort of trapdoor. I had hit my head on the way down. It still hurt a bit. Otherwise I was okay. Beneath me was an old mattress on a rusted frame. It had broken my fall.

Above me was the hole I'd fallen through. And Simon, shining his light on me.

"It's about time you woke up," he shouted. "Are you okay?"

"I guess so."

"Can you get out?"

"Shine your light around so I can look for my flashlight."

My flashlight had rolled only a short distance away. I found it, gave it a good shake, then shone it around the room.

Just your basic, plain old jail cell, lined with bars—and no way to escape. The floor of my cell was about eight feet from the ceiling.

"Looks like I'm going to have to climb out that trapdoor," I told Simon. "Throw me down the rope."

"What rope?"

"The rope in your backpack."

"I thought it was your turn to bring rope."

Simon was right. It was my turn. Which meant we had forgotten the rope back at my house. I got so mad that I banged my fist against one of the steel bars.

It snapped in two.

So did the next three that I hit. In fact, the whole jail cell broke quicker than a sharpened pencil point during a math exam.

That's one good thing about rust, I guess.

"I won't need the rope," I called back. "At least not yet. I'm going to look for a way out of here. You go and check those other rooms off the hallway."

"Gotcha."

Across from the jail cell was a jungle of tubes and some vats, a lot like what you'd see in a laboratory.

Had I stumbled into a mad scientist's workplace?

I continued to explore, and soon found a ramp that seemed to lead to the outside. Light filtered through a few beat-up boards.

But I wasn't ready to leave just yet. I pushed back through the basement cobwebs. The place had a funny smell—a little like our garage when my dad hasn't taken the soda bottles back for a while.

A closet door sat in the wall on the other side of the lab equipment. A skeleton closet, maybe? A place where the scientist kept experiments that didn't work out?

The batteries in my flashlight were getting weaker

and weaker. The light went from white to yellow as I approached the door.

I was about ten feet away when I heard something moving in the closet. I thought of yelling for Simon, but realized that might scare off what ever was behind that door.

Or warn it I was coming.

My flashlight flickered off, batteries dead. It didn't matter. The ghost film would record whatever was there, dark or light.

And there was something definitely there. I could hardly see in the pitch blackness, but I could hear just fine. And what I heard was banging.

Then the sound of doorknob turning.

This was it. I pushed the camera in front of my face just as the door flew open.

"Gotcha!" I shouted, pressing the camera button.

"Got who?" said Simon, blinding me with his commando light. He'd found the basement stairs.

Needless to say, we were both disappointed. And tired. Ghost hunting takes a lot out of you.

"I think we should call it a day," suggested Simon. "Let's go over to World of Stuff and get a Black Cow."

I had to agree. We trudged up the basement ramp and pushed away the boards. Then we marched through some overgrown weeds along the side of the house. In a few minutes we were taking our usual spots at the World of Stuff soda fountain.

"You boys look a little down in the dumps," said Mr. Radford, twitching his mustache at us. "Got just the thing for you: double shots of Black Cow."

"Make mine a triple," I said.

"Coming right up."

"Say, Mr. Radford, has anyone ever told you that you look a lot like Gomez on the *Addams Family?*"

"No. Why do you ask?"

I shrugged. "No reason."

"He's a handsome guy, I'll bet."

I nodded. Mr. Radford went back to making our drinks.

One thing about Black Cows: They sure do hit the spot. I emptied my glass in about three seconds flat and pushed it forward for a refill.

"What have you guys been up to today?" Mr. Radford asked.

"The usual," said Simon. "Looking for ghosts. We went over to the Gambino house."

Mr. Radford smiled. "Ah yes, haunted house number twenty-six. The old Gambino casino. One of my favorites."

"Casino? So that's why there was a roulette wheel," I said.

"A crooked roulctte wheel," said Mr. Radford. "Don't play any number other than thirteen."

"I thought gambling was against the law," said Simon.

"Oh, it is. But the place has been haunted since Prohibition ended. It was a speakeasy."

Mr. Radford explained that Prohibition was a time during the 1920s. Drinking alcohol was against the law. Even so, a lot of people did it. They would go to secret, illegal clubs called speakeasies. Besides drinking, all sorts of things went on there, including gambling.

In those days, gangsters roamed the streets doing battle with FBI agents, who were called G-man. The *G* stood for government. The head of the FBI, J. Edgar Hoover, launched a war against gangsters, and put a lot of them in jail.

Mr. Radford acted out a fight between the G-men and the gangsters, practically knocking over our drinks.

"Easy!" I shouted, grabbing my Black Cow.

"Sorry," he said. He took his cloth and began wiping the counter. "The Gambino casino. Boy, the parties they had. If those walls could talk . . . Well, they do talk. But if they couldn't and they could, they would have some stories to tell, except they wouldn't."

Mr. Radford is a great guy, but not everything he says makes sense, I thought as I wondered what he meant.

"Is the Gambino place haunted?" Simon asked.

"They wouldn't call it haunted house number twenty-six if it wasn't."

"We didn't see any ghosts," I said. "We can't put it in our survey of haunted houses unless we have absolute proof."

"Maybe they didn't want you to see them," said Mr. Radford. "Ghosts are funny like that sometimes. They won't show themselves for just anyone."

"There ought to be special ghost glasses to let you see ghosts," said Simon. "Then you could see them whether they wanted you to see them or not."

"I had a dream about that, in the house," I said, remembering. "Is there such a thing?"

"Never heard of ghost glasses. I'm sure I'd carry them if they existed. Got plenty of eyeglasses, though. And wine glasses. Want to buy some of those?"

"I don't think so," said Simon.

"We saw a door with some writing on it," I told Mr. Radford. "Do you know who the 'Naughty Nannies' were?"

"Oh, ho, ho. The Naughty Nannies." Mr. Radford smiled and did a funny thing with his head, wagging it back and forth like he had told himself a joke. Then he winked. Meanwhile, his face turned red, like he was embarrassed. "Burlesque. I don't think you boys are old enough for the Naughty Nannies."

"What are they?"

"Oh, ho, ho. I don't think I should say. Don't want to get you too interested. Wait until you're twenty-one. Or in probate court, which ever comes first."

I didn't exactly know what he meant, but I could guess from the winking. Being that Simon was still a kid, I changed the subject.

"Come on Simon, let's get back home. My mom left some frozen dinners for lunch."

"Not turnips again," he moaned.

"Don't worry, I got her off that kick. Nothing but lasagna and octopus lips from now on."

"Octopus lips?"

"Just kidding."

"Too bad."

I'd forgotten all about the package for Uncle Fred until I turned the corner and saw a bright purple van pulling away from our house. On the side of the van were the words DREAM DELIVERIES.

It took another second for me to realize that the driver had not taken the package for my uncle. It was still sitting on the front step. By then the van was too far away for the driver to hear my shouts. I tried chasing after him but I was too exhausted from my morning's exploration to catch up.

"Hey, what's with the box?" Simon asked as I joined him on the lawn.

"Oh, that's just the dumb clock my uncle sent. I guess the guy needed me to sign something before he would take it."

"No, that package near the door. The one behind the bushes."

Sure enough, there was a big box there. A purple label slashed across it.

DREAM DELIVERIES, read the label.

"What do you think it is?" Simon asked.

"Got me. Probably a mix-up. The driver dropped something off instead of making a pickup."

"But it's got your name on it."

So it did. I had Simon help me drag it over to the front lawn. I borrowed his pocket knife and slit it open.

There was a giant toothbrush inside. Just like the one that had chased me in my dream.

"Hey, there's another box back here," said Simon. He picked up a box that was about the size of a wastepaper basket. "What do you think is in here?"

"Probably toothpaste to go with this," I said. "It

31

must be my mom's idea of a joke. I'll bet she had them deliver this to remind me to brush my teeth. Eerie has gotten to her. She's finally cracked.''

But there wasn't any toothpaste in the box at all.

Instead there were two dozen pairs of eyeglasses, in all shapes and sizes. And each one had a tag that read:

GHOST GLASSES. GUARANTEED TO LET YOU SEE THE SPECTER OF YOUR CHOICE.

4

We were so excited, and so hungry, that we wolfed lunch down in about two seconds.

Cooking it had been another story. As soon as I had closed the microwave door, the platter inside began spinning around at full speed. Our frozen lunches of ham, peas and potatoes shot all over the inside of the machine. I ended up scooping the bits out with a spoon. Everything was swirled together like stew.

Simon liked that. I didn't care. I was too busy planning what to do if the glasses really worked. It was going to be a great summer.

As soon as we finished eating Simon put a few pairs of ghost glasses in a shoebox to take home and we put all but two of the rest into the Evidence Locker. We headed back to haunted house number twenty-six, aka (also known as) the Gambino casino. My hands trembled as we walked up the front steps. I handed Simon my backpack. Then I took a deep breath and put on the glasses.

Nothing looked any different. The chipped gray paint on the door was just as chipped as before, and just as gray. Slowly I turned the knob and pushed. The hinges moaned, but the hallway seemed even emptier than before.

"Turn on the laser light and follow me," I told Simon, taking a baby step inside. Still nothing.

I poked my head inside the room where Simon had heard the noise earlier.

Not even a shadow of a shadow.

"You see anything?" whispered Simon behind me.

"Nope."

"Me, neither. Maybe Mr. Radford was right—there is no such thing as ghost glasses."

"Tags can't lie, Simon. Haven't you ever heard of truth in advertising?"

He didn't have an answer for that. I crept down the hallway. The hole leading into the secret gambling room was ahead on my left.

You can't live in Eerie very long without running into a ghost or two. Most of them aren't all that scary. In fact, I'd be willing to bet that ghosts are among the most normal people in Eerie. But there are always one or two who spoil the apple bin, if you know what I mean. A sour McIntosh that gives the pie a bad name.

Those are the kinds of ghosts that scare me. And you

never know when you're going to find one. I paused at the hole in the wall, not sure what I would find.

"Well, are you going inside or not?" demanded Simon.

"Don't rush me." I took one last breath and slipped through.

There were ghosts in here all right. A lot of ghosts. A crowded room full of ghosts. Women in party dresses, giggling and smoking. Guys in tuxedoes, laughing and drinking. Cards flew and the roulette wheel spun.

There were more ghosts here than I'd seen in my entire life, added together and multiplied by five.

I tried waving at one or two of them. They didn't seem to notice me. *Maybe they needed people glasses to see me,* I thought.

I took a step forward into the room. Then something tugged my arm. I was so startled I jumped—and the glasses fell off.

It was only Simon. I blinked as I looked at him. The room was empty, as empty as that morning.

"Well, do they work?" asked Simon, who was also wearing a pair of ghost glasses.

"Can't you tell?"

"My eyes are closed."

"Open them and see," I said, putting my glasses back on.

"Wow!" he said, following me into the room. "Wow!"

All the ghosts seemed to be having a great time. A lot of them were drinking from glasses with long stems and a kind of triangular top. There were olives in their glasses, and I think their drinks were called martinis. A bunch of waiters walked around the room with them on their trays, and people grabbed the glasses as they passed. Ghosts in fancy clothes kneeled down on the floor to roll dice in the corner.

Simon and I stood in the middle of the room for at least five minutes, watching everything around us. Ghosts walked right through us as if we weren't there. It was almost like being in the middle of a movie. We were so awed by it all that I forgot I had brought the camera.

Finally I remembered. I pointed it toward the roulette wheel and took a shot. Then I pointed it in the other direction and took another.

I waited eagerly while the film developed. In another second, I thought, we'd have proof.

Wrong. When the images appeared, the photos were exactly like the ones I had taken before. No ghosts.

"Simon, look at this. There aren't any ghosts in the pictures."

"Maybe you need to put the ghost glasses in front of the lens."

"Good idea," I said. "Give me your glasses."

"*My* glasses? What about yours?"

"Come on, quit arguing. I have to see to focus."

He sighed, then took one last look around the room. "Here," he said. "Then let's go check out that 'Naughty Nannies' room."

"I think we'll wait for that." I put the glasses in front of the lens. I was trying to figure out how to hold the camera and the glasses and still press the button to take the picture when I heard a woman shriek.

"What are those kids doing in here!"

I looked up and saw a ghost in a gold-spangled dress pointing at me.

"They're looking at us!" shouted another ghost.

"The nerve!"

"I hate it when people look at us!"

Up until now, we hadn't been able to hear them talk. All of a sudden, we couldn't shut them up. Everyone was shouting. Drinks dropped. Then I heard the words, "Get them!" from the back of the room.

"Time to go," I told Simon, heading toward the wall and its opening.

He was already two steps in front of me.

"I'll teach you to look at ghosts," said a deep voice

37

behind me. I glanced back and saw a ghost in a white tuxedo shoot across the room. A mustache curled beneath his massive red nose. The mustache looked like the handlebars on a bicycle, only thicker. His eyes sparkled with anger as he flew. "I'll give you a haunting you won't forget!" he hissed.

Then something picked me up by the back of my shirt. Suddenly I was flying through the air. Simon was right beside me.

How loud do you think you could scream if a ghost grabbed hold of you? Louder than a fire engine? Louder than a jet taking off? Louder than your sister when you filled her shampoo bottle with purple food dye?

Simon and I screamed so loud our lungs hurt. Whatever had grabbed us hurtled us toward the back wall of the speakeasy.

Lucky for us, it was made out of cardboard, like the other wall. We shot right through, into a room that looked a lot like a library.

Unlucky for us, we kept going—right through the bookcases on the far side.

The books were more pieces of cardboard. The entire library was fake. But we didn't stop there—we shot right through two broken windows and plopped into a pond in the backyard.

A scummy, slimy pond, about ten times smellier than a sewer hole.

"That was pretty exciting," said Simon as we pulled ourselves out of the pool. "Those glasses really work."

"I'll say."

I looked around as I tried to wring out my T-shirt. Whatever had thrown us out here had decided to leave us alone. At least for now.

I still had the camera because it had been tied to a strap around my neck. But we had lost our glasses. And I was in no mood to go back inside and find them.

"Did the picture come out?" Simon asked.

"I didn't even get a chance to take it, before that lady saw us."

"Well, at least we know the place is haunted."

"Of course we know," I answered. "But we have to be able to prove it to other people. People outside of Eerie, who won't think it's normal. We're back where we started."

"No, we're not," he said. "All we have to do is lend someone a pair of the ghost glasses. Then they'll see for themselves."

"That's not going to work. They'll think it's a trick. Besides, we need proof that we can put in a book, like a photograph. I wonder where the glasses came from, anyway.''

Simon bent over and pulled an angelfish from his pocket. He looked at it for a moment, then tossed it back into the water.

''Maybe Mr. Radford found them and sent them over. We were talking about them at World of Stuff.''

''Maybe,'' I agreed. ''But if so, they came awful fast. And besides, that doesn't explain the toothbrush.''

''I thought your mom sent it.''

''I don't know about that.''

I already had an idea about where the glasses and toothbrush had come from. I had dreamed about a tooth-brush and ghost glasses when I was knocked out. And the name of the delivery company was Dream Deliveries.

Now, no normal person would think a delivery service can just bring made-up things to your door, especially if these things don't exist.

Unless, of course, you live in Eerie, Indiana.

5

Simon didn't believe me at first about where the glasses and toothbrush had come from. He's like that sometimes. He likes to say that he was born in Oklahoma, which is the "Show me" state.

He wasn't born there at all, but he likes to say that. It means he wants proof before he believes what you tell him.

So the first thing we did was go over to World of Stuff, to make sure Mr. Radford hadn't sent the glasses over.

He looked at us with bug eyes when I asked. Either he hadn't, or a scientist had injected bug DNA into his body.

Next, we headed over to the library to try and find out what we could about ghost glasses. The Para-almost-normal section is in the library's new wing. It

41

was built with a grant from the Society for the Preservation of UFO Sightings. It's a pretty neat part of the library, except for the flashing lights and whirring sounds.

We thumbed through the card catalog, looking for ghost glasses. There were books on ghost gadflies and ghost goulashes, but no ghost glasses.

"Maybe it's in one of the ghost-hunting handbooks," Simon whispered.

Well, all right, he didn't exactly whisper. When Simon gets an idea, he gets excited. And when he's excited he shouts.

One of the librarians, Mrs. Piddlefeather, came running to shush us. Mrs. Piddlefeather is about ninety years old and weighs close to five hundred pounds, so she didn't run very fast. But you could hear her all the way from the Poison Plants section. When she shushes someone, she sounds like a vacuum cleaner with something caught in the nozzle.

"SSSSSSSHHHHHH! SSSSSSSHHHHHH!" she said.

Simon apologized. Mrs. Piddlefeather isn't a bad person, really. She just likes things quiet in the library. "Quiet enough to hear the dead," she insists. "And the dead only murmur—they never shout."

"We're sorry for the noise," I told her.

She took off her glasses and scanned us from top to bottom. "What are you boys looking for, anyway?"

"We're trying to see if there are any books on ghost glasses," I told her.

"Ghost glasses? You mean like a service station that gives out presents with a fill-up? If you go into a haunted house, you get a glass?"

"That'd be a good idea," I said. "But that wasn't what we meant."

"Ghost eyeglasses," explained Simon. "You know—glasses that you can see ghosts with."

"Oh, ghost glasses," she nodded. "No such thing."

"How do you know?" he asked.

"There aren't any books on them."

"But that doesn't mean they don't exist," I said.

She made a noise that sounded like her throat was exploding. Then she put her glasses back on and examined the card catalog. You could tell she really knew what she was doing. Her fingers flew through it like they weren't attached to her hands.

"Here we go—Odd Ghost Hunting Paraphernalia," she said, pulling a card out. She read it. "See *Unusual,* see *Weird,* see *Stuff You Wouldn't Believe in a Million Years.* Let's see, that would be down with the speculative fiction."

Mrs. Piddlefeather led the way to a set of bookshelves several levels below, in the basement. At the far end of the farthest wall, she found the bookcase she wanted. Pulling over a ladder, she climbed up to the top shelf. There she retrieved a book that looked almost brand-new—once she blew the dust off the cover. *Ghost Stuff That You Wish You Had, but Don't* was the title.

Quickly, she flipped through the book. "Here we go!" she announced triumphantly. "A whole chapter on ghost glasses."

It was the shortest chapter in the book. The whole thing was one sentence: "Ghost glasses—no such thing."

That didn't totally convince Simon, but it got him halfway there. What drove him the rest of the way was the red 1965 Mustang convertible that appeared in our driveway the next morning.

Needless to say, it was exactly like the one my dad said he was going to dream about: red, with a V-8 engine and a three-speed stick shift. It even had an eight-track tape player.

An eight-track is an old-fashioned kind of cassette deck, only different. It can only play songs from groups like the Partridge Family and the BeeGees. I'm not really up on my geezer rock, but I think they were part of a secret weapon used by the enemy during the Cold War. Fortunately, the CIA found out and invented acid rock as an antidote.

When my dad found the tag on the steering wheel with his name on it, he concluded that his company had sent it to him as an early Christmas bonus.

And I do mean early. Like six months. I guess you believe what you want to believe.

The car wasn't the only thing that showed up after someone in the family had a dream. Remember what my sister Syndi said about a "dreamboat"? Between you and me, I think she meant a boyfriend. But whoever was handling the dream delivery system took it word for word. The S. S. Dreamboat, a forty-five-foot cabin cruiser, was parked on our lawn the afternoon Dad's car arrived.

Syndi figured it was some sort of a mistake. Even so, she decided it would be okay if she took it down to Lake Eerie for a ride before giving it back.

Fortunately, Dad's new car had a trailer hitch attached. We all went for a cruise that very afternoon.

Even Mom got something she dreamed about—a brand-new combination toaster microwave juice blender and potato masher, all in one. No more toast crushed on the ceiling, no more spun-out frozen dinners.

45

Uncle Fred's present stayed on the front stoop. In all the excitement, it kind of got forgotten.

If this dream delivery business had ended right there, everything would have been fantastic.

But if it had, it wouldn't have been Eerie.

6

The funny thing is, I didn't have any dreams for the next few days—at least none that I could remember. Stuff kept coming for my parents and sister. A couple of times I almost told them what was happening, but I knew they wouldn't believe me. Besides, they were having fun playing with their new toys—Dad especially. He spent a whole hour in the driveway, sitting in his Mustang. He pressed a button and watched the top fold down into the back. Then he'd push it again and watch it swing up into place.

"Works like a dream every time," he said. He didn't know how right he was.

The only one not having fun was Syndi. Her driving classes weren't going too well. She kept flunking the practice exams. She did okay on multiple-choice questions. For example:

If you're driving down a state highway and see a bat sitting in the middle of the road, you should:

47

a) get out of the car and help it across.
b) yield the right of way.
c) speed up.
d) check your rearview mirror for vampires.

The answer is (b) yield the right of way. It's kind of a trick question, because if you were in Eerie instead of on a state highway, you would (d) check your rearview mirror for vampires.

They sure take their driving seriously in Eerie.

A few mornings later Mom was making breakfast in the kitchen with her new toaster/microwave/juicer/potato masher. She had bought these frozen fruit bagels at World of Stuff, and decided to try them out on me. They came in different flavors: banana, pumpkin, and watermelon. She plopped a banana bagel into the machine and pressed the switch. In thirty seconds a buzzer sounded and out poured a glass of fruit-bagel juice.

"Oh darn, I pushed the wrong button again," said my mom, looking at the glass. "Oh well, it all ends up in the same place anyway. Here you go, Marshall."

Surprisingly, it didn't taste all that bad. In fact, I was just about to ask for a glass of pumpkin bagel when the front door flew open. Dad stormed into the house, grumbling under his breath. He walked into the kitchen and started turning off lights.

"Edgar, what are you doing?" demanded my mother as he pulled the radio plug out of the socket.

"Look at this electric bill! It's over seven thousand dollars!" exclaimed my father. He threw the bill down on the table and continued pulling plugs. "We have to cut back!"

I picked up the bill. It was for $7,564.13, to be exact.

It had come in an envelope marked DREAM DELIVERIES.

"I had a nightmare about this last night," said my father, reaching for the plug to the toaster/microwave/juicer/potato masher.

"Not my new machine!" cried my mom, throwing her arms across it.

But it was too late. Dad cut the power mid-bagel. Then he went to the refrigerator and started pulling it away from the wall.

"If you do that, all the food will go bad," said my mom.

"We'll just have to do without."

"What about milk for your coffee?"

"I'll take powdered."

"I was going to make spaghetti and meatballs tonight. If you cut the power, the meat will spoil before I can cook it."

After Swedish cutlets, spaghetti and meatballs was my dad's favorite dish in the world.

"The refrigerator goes off after dinner," he said, pushing it back. Then he marched out of the kitchen to look for other plugs to pull.

Just then there was a knock on the kitchen door. I got up from the table and opened the door, only to find a gorilla in an army uniform standing there.

And I'm not exaggerating.

"You Syndi Teller?" demanded the gorilla.

I was so startled I barely remembered how to shake my head no.

"Come on, come on, I don't have all day," said the gorilla, barging into the house. "I'm her new driving instructor. Where is she?"

Syndi chose that moment to walk into the kitchen. She ran out a half second later, screaming that her nightmare had come true.

"Excuse me, sir," said my mom. "But you're tracking your boots all through my kitchen. I just mopped up."

"So? You want a medal?" said the gorilla.

"I want you to wait outside in the driveway."

"Women," he said, shaking his head. He took a step back toward the door. "All right, listen. I don't know which one of you is Syndi Teller, but she has five min-

50

utes to meet me in the car, or I'm leaving. I'll be outside, practicing my screams."

"The nerve," said my mom, grabbing her mop from the pantry.

This had gone far enough. I knew I had to do something to stop Dream Deliveries, but I wasn't sure what. I decided to start by telling my parents what was going on.

"Listen, Mom, there's something I have to tell you. Remember that package for Uncle Fred?"

"Now there's someone at the *front* door," said my mom as the doorbell drowned out my words. "Marshall, honey, would you answer it?"

"But there's something I have to tell you first. All the stuff that's been coming to the house, see—"

"Marshall, please, can't you see I'm in a crisis here? I have to mop up the kitchen floor, replug in all the appliances, and get ready for work, all in three minutes. I haven't even picked out what I want to wear yet. Can't you please answer the door? It's all I ask."

Sighing, I went to find out who was ringing the bell. It's times like this when I wished I was back in New Jersey. There, all I had to worry about was living over a toxic waste dump and the high crime rate.

"Special delivery for Marilyn Teller," announced the man in the purple uniform at the door.

"Hey, you're from Dream Deliveries, aren't you?" I asked.

Actually, I didn't ask that at all. I tried to. I started to. But before I got half of the *Hey* out of my mouth, the man dropped a huge, squishy package into my arms. It was so heavy I fell backwards into the house. Before I knew what was happening, he dropped three more on me.

Struggling for air, I rolled and clawed my way free. Back on my feet, I hopped out the door and tried to stop the guy. But all I saw was the back of a purple van, vanishing into the distance.

"What is all this, Marshall?" came my mom's voice from inside. "They look like the big clothes containers dry cleaners use."

The next thing I heard was my mom's scream of terror.

"**A**ll of my clothes, ruined! Ripped, stained and shredded!" screamed my mom. "This is horrible! A nightmare."

The living room looked something like a rag pile after a tornado had blown through. Every piece of clothing Mom owned, except for the robe and pajamas she was wearing, was destroyed. She pulled them in tatters from the bags. Some disintegrated in her hands. Others were covered with streaks and stains. Car grease, strawberry jam, the stuff that squishes out when you crush a bug— you name it, it was there. A few things had shrunk to such a small size they looked like doll clothes. I never knew there were so many ways clothes could be destroyed.

I didn't have to ask if she had dreamed about it recently.

"Mom, there's something I have to tell you. Dream Deliveries—"

"Not now, Marshall," she said, jumping to her feet. "What am I going to wear? Syndi? Syndi!"

Mom ran upstairs to see if she could borrow something from my sister. I went to the kitchen and called Dream Deliveries.

Busy.

I pressed *O* for operator.

A woman's voice answered right away. "Operator. May I help you?"

"I have to talk to Dream Deliveries," I told her.

"Young man, have you tried dialing their number?"

"Yes, but it's busy."

"You'll just have to try again."

"But it's always busy. Can't you do something?"

"Who do you think I am? The phone company?"

"Yes!"

"Oh. So I am. Good day."

And with that, she hung up.

I tried dialing back, but now the operator's line was busy, too. Desperate, I grabbed the phone book. I hoped there might be another number for Dream Deliveries, or maybe an address.

Nope.

Dad was still stomping around the house, unplugging stuff. I could hear Mom groan as she tried to squeeze inside one of Syndi's dresses. Syndi was upstairs crying on her bed, sobbing that she was never going to get her driver's permit. Outside, the gorilla driving instructor was still working on his screams. His voice shook the kitchen windows.

"You call that parallel parking? I've seen cab drivers who drive better than you do!"

I needed to go someplace where I could think. I ripped the page out of the phone book with the Dream Deliveries phone number. Picking my way through the clothes in the living room, I bolted out the front door and made a beeline for Simon's house.

Do you ever wonder why they call it a beeline? It's supposed to mean you go straight without stopping, right? But bees never go straight anywhere, not even in Eerie. They zip here, zip there, smell this flower, taste that pollen. Bees are about the most crooked traveling insects I know.

Just something to think about.

I found Simon sitting on the back porch of his house. Scattered around the back lawn were thousands of plastic soldiers, along with little plastic tanks, artillery guns and some toy airplanes. There were enough soldiers there to fight World War III.

"Hey, Simon, we need to do something."

"*Ssshhh*—I'm counting."

Simon's still a little kid, so it's only natural that he likes to play with toy soldiers and stuff.

"Dream Deliveries is now sending nightmares to my house," I told him. "I have to get them to stop."

"Drat, Marshall—I was just figuring out how many *liers* I have. Now I have to count all over."

"Liars?"

"Liers. You know. Lying down guys."

"Come on, I need your help. We have to find out where this Dream Deliveries place is and get them to stop."

Simon sighed. "How?"

"I don't know." I had to push away a pile of toy soldiers to sit down. Then I took the page from the phone book out of my pocket. "All that's in their ad is the phone number."

Simon studied it. "Maybe there's kind of a reverse phone book," he suggested. "Where you could look up a phone number and find the address."

That's why I like Simon so much. For a little kid, he's got a great brain. I slapped him on the back and we jumped off the porch. We made a beeline—no, better call it a "train line"—for the Eerie Library, where we discovered there was no such thing as a reverse telephone book.

"There is a service on the Eerie Net you can try," said the librarian, leading the way to the library's computer.

I know you've heard of the Internet. Most likely you've tried it a few times yourself. Well, the "Eerie Net" is Eerie's own special version of the Internet. You want to talk about web pages? We've got *real* web pages.

There is one slight problem. The Eerie Net computer is located in a telephone booth under the stairs in the library basement. To fit there, the telephone booth had to be put on its side. That means to use it, you sit upside down on your back with your feet in the air. Otherwise, it's much better than a regular computer.

There is no keyboard or mouse. Instead, you speak commands into a telephone receiver. The Eerie Net computer is smart enough to follow the directions.

But that isn't the best part. You know how most computers have video screens that show you the words? Some screens are big, some are flat, some are just two colors? Well, the Eerie Net computer doesn't have a screen at all. When you go inside, a round dome clamps over your head. The dome looks a little like an old-fashioned hairdryer in a beauty parlor. The computer images are flashed right inside your brain.

I don't know how it all works, or why Eerie, of all

places, has this advanced system. The only hookup is at the town library. It's about twelve hundred times faster than any ordinary Internet connection. Of course, since you are upside down, you can't use it for very long. All the blood rushes to your head. Even if you can stand the headache, the blood interferes with the video transmission.

I climbed into the phone booth and waited for the computer to boot up. It played reveille, then recited the Pledge of Allegiance, and finally played the theme song from an old Bugs Bunny cartoon backwards. When that was done, the words WELCOME TO EERIE NET, MARSHALL, flickered in front of my face.

"I need to know the address of Dream Deliveries," I said.

I'M SORRY, came the computer's reply. THAT ADDRESS IS UNLISTED.

"How can that be?"

WHO KNOWS? wrote the computer. WHY DO THEY CALL IT A BEELINE WHEN IT'S MORE LIKE A CRAZY, TANGLED CURVE?

I tried asking a bunch more questions, but still didn't get an address or another phone number. The day was a complete bust. Simon and I tried calling the Dream Deliveries phone number about a million different times from a million different phone booths.

Busy. Always busy.

My house was dark when I got home. Not because it was so late or empty, but because Dad had turned off all the lights. Inside the kitchen, Mom was making dinner by candlelight. She was wearing one of Syndi's cheerleader outfits. Tonight was Italian night. She had a little trouble making the meatballs. They kept squirting off the counter and getting lost in the shadows.

My sister sat at the table, writing out a practice answer for her driver's permit. I peeked over her shoulder and saw the question:

Write an essay explaining how green a green light should be. (5 pages)

She had already filled two sheets of paper.

"What did you do today, Marshall?" my mom asked.

"I tried to call Dream Deliveries."

"Dream Deliveries? You mean the people who were supposed to come and get Uncle Fred's present? They never came. It's still on the porch."

"Mom! Why do you think all this weird stuff has been happening around here? Where do you think Dad's Mustang came from? And Syndi's boat?"

"You don't have to shout. I can hear you. I can't see you, but I can hear you."

"All this stuff that's been delivered to the house," I

said. "It's all from Dream Deliveries. Now they're sending over nightmares."

"Then why didn't they pick up Uncle Fred's package?"

"Because they're in the delivery business. They only deliver, Mom. Dreams. Everything that's come, it's been something one of us dreamed about. The car, the boat. Even your ruined clothes. You had a nightmare about that, right?"

"The dry cleaner just messed up, that's all. I plan to go over there tomorrow and straighten it all out."

"But you never sent all your clothes out to the dry cleaner, did you?"

"Marshall, you know they make regular pickups. I'm sure that they just made a mistake. Probably a new person was working that day."

"*Ssshhh*, both of you," scolded my sister. "How do you expect me to study with you jabbering away?"

It was useless to try and explain. It was like everything else in Eerie—no one believed me. Check that. They believed me all right. They just didn't think what I told them was weird. Like having Elvis as your neighbor. Or Bigfoot going through your trash. It was all normal. It was all Eerie. And it was only going to get worse.

*E*ating dinner was frustrating. There was only one candle on the table, and it was hard to see what I was doing. I would twirl my spaghetti until I figured I had it all. But when I put it in my mouth, all I got was a forkful of air.

Plus my mom had miscalculated on how much food to make. I mean, seriously miscalculated. There was hardly enough spaghetti for one person, let alone four. And we could only find two meatballs in the sauce. I left the table hungrier than I had started.

Even so, the rest of the family seemed to be in a good mood. They had decided that the disasters of the morning would work themselves out. That was just the way my family was.

My father decided that he would speak to the electric company about the bill. Maybe there was a budget plan or something. In the meantime, we would keep as much electricity off as possible. That meant no TV, no video or computer games, no stereo even. But it also meant that I didn't have to watch my mom's programs, play my dad's ancient Atari Pong game, or listen to Syndi's sappy music. All in all, not a bad deal.

We huddled around one candle, reading. Dad had the latest copy of *Antimatter Times*, one of the magazines he always reads for work. He spent most of the night looking at an article called "The Universe: God Playing Dice, or Is It a Card Game?"

Mom read a romance novel. Syndi studied her driver's manual. And I was busy thumbing through the phone book, trying to see if Dream Deliveries was listed under a different name.

I learned it's not very exciting, reading a phone book. I was hoping to find the exact same number listed. Then I would have the address. You know, kind of like a reverse phone book.

I knew it wasn't going to work after the first page. Still, I kept going. I'm stubborn like that sometimes. My eyelids got heavier and heavier as I went. Finally, they fell over my eyes like lead weights sinking a fishing line. The next thing I knew, my dad was shaking my shoulder.

"Time for bed, champ. Tomorrow's another day."

You know how sometimes your head hits the pillow and you fall right to sleep? Not just any kind of sleep—

deep, deep sleep. Like you're floating on a cloud, and there's nothing around. Or in the middle of a warm, warm ocean. There's no noise. Everything is peaceful. You feel happier than you can imagine. Happier than if your favorite football team won the Super Bowl. Happier than if you were struggling to ride a bike up a hill and discovered that it had ten more gears. Happier than you would be if you won a gift certificate for a million dollars from Toys Я Us.

Deep, peaceful sleep. The most restful, perfect sleep in the world.

Do you know that sleep?

So do I. And let me tell you, I sure didn't sleep that way. Even though I had dozed off downstairs, I could not get comfortable when I went to bed. My stomach growled. All I could think of was food. Vats of spaghetti, meatballs, huge pizza pies, even veal parmigiana, floated in front of my eyes.

I lay my head on the pillow and tried to go back to dreamsville. I thought to myself, "Wouldn't it be great to dream this stuff, and find it here in the morning?"

Running. I was running. My heart beat faster than a drum roll. Bullets flew past my head.

I was being chased by a band of mobsters through my living room. Which changed into the Gambino casino. Except it was filled with people. Most were laughing and dancing.

The others were chasing me.

I ducked down the hallway and through one of the rooms where people were gambling. One of the gangsters was right behind me. He was so close I could smell his stench. My stomach just about turned. Then I felt him grab the back of my shirt.

Desperate, I twisted away. He lost his grip, but still managed to knock me off balance. I flew headfirst into one of the tables. Everything went flying. Scrambling to my feet, I saw another gangster coming at me from the other side. Like an otter diving into the water, I nosed down under the roulette table. He tried to follow, but crashed into the table instead.

I searched the floor for the trapdoor but couldn't find it. Bullets rang through the room like a hard summer's hail. I jumped back up and ran to a panel at the wall that connected with the fake library. Still no switch for the trapdoor. The gangsters kept up the chase.

Somehow I made it to the front hallway, only to find the door blocked by the fattest, meanest-looking gangster this side of Al Capone. He wore a lime green suit and looked about as attractive as a magpie.

"I've been waiting for you, Marshall," he said,

thumping his chest with his thumb. "I'm Mr. Linguine. But you can call me Lefty."

His cold fingers clamped me around the neck, and began to squeeze.

9

I woke up with a scream. The dream had been so vivid, I thought it was real. I didn't calm down for at least five minutes.

When I did, I realized how much trouble I was in.

How much trouble everybody was in.

It was still dark outside. Up until now, the Dream Deliveries van had always waited until dawn to make its drop-offs. So I had some time, but I couldn't be sure how much. When Dad unplugged everything, he got to my clock, too.

The first thing I could think of—in fact, the only thing I could think of—was to get out of the house. I jumped out of bed, got dressed, and left. All I took with me was the emergency bag of M&Ms I kept under the bed in case I got really hungry. Then I decided to grab some change in case I got hungrier.

I wasn't running away. Until now, all of the deliveries

had been made to the house when the person who dreamed them was home. Somehow, the delivery van timed it just right. You were either just getting home, or busy inside.

So I figured, if I wasn't at the house they wouldn't deliver there. My family would be spared.

But that still left me in a whole anthill's worth of trouble.

Even in Eerie, two heads are better than one—unless they're attached. So I went over to Simon's house next door. His place was locked up tighter than a casket—a lot tighter than any caskets in *this* town, anyway. I tried throwing little pebbles at his window to wake him up. He must not have heard them. Finally I decided it wasn't safe to wait around any longer. I didn't want the van to deliver its gangsters to Simon's house.

Eerie at night is even stranger than during the day. There's usually a Wolves' Club meeting going on at the town green, across from Eerie General Hospital. Fortunately, their howls are worse than their bites. Then there are the worms. If you walk down Bug Lane, the block behind Eerie Bait Shop and Sushi Bar, you can hardly take a step on the sidewalk without squishing a nightcrawler.

When I got to Main Street, I realized there was an easy solution to my problem. The delivery van would find me no matter where I was, right? So I should go to a good place for capturing gangsters—which meant the police station.

Great idea. Except when it came to explaining why I was there.

"Gangsters? In Eerie?" Sergeant Knight smirked and leaned over his desk at the dispatch window. "Come on, kid. Tell me something I believe."

"Let me just sit here for a while and they'll come. I swear. See, there's this company called Dream Deliveries, and—"

"Hey, aren't you the Teller kid? You're one of the boys who was messing with that ATM machine, aren't you? Right before it started giving out money. Come here, I want to talk to you—"

I didn't hang around to hear the rest of what he said. A few weeks before, Simon had made friends with Mr. Wilson, the new ATM my dad was testing at the Eerie Savings and Loan. It started spewing out money. There was a big scandal in town. Simon and I put all the money back. We hadn't done anything wrong, but Sergeant Knight didn't look like he was in an understanding mood.

So I let my sneakers do the talking. I dodged out of the police station and headed uptown to the Eerie Bus Terminal and Supper Club. The terminal was open all night. I thought I might be able to find a place to hide for a while. Then when the bad guys came looking for me, someone was sure to call the police. I'd be able to escape, and this little nightmare would be over.

In the waiting room I found a vending machine that dispensed chocolate drinks, potato chips and disguises. I put in four quarters and got a set of fake eyeglasses with a mustache. Then I found a spot to hide: between the big scale and the fortune-teller booth.

All in all, I'd have to say my plan was an excellent one—except that the gangsters never showed up.

The terminal clock read 7 A.M. It was about time to do my paper route. But was it safe?

Maybe. Nothing bad had happened all night. Unless you count the lady who slugged the big scale when it told her she weighed one hundred and seventy-five pounds.

I decided to take a look around outside. Part of me worried that the gangsters were waiting in gangster cars on the street. The other part was starting to have doubts about the whole thing. Maybe I had been wrong about Dream Deliveries. Maybe everything that had happened was a coincidence. After all, my dad's company *did* sometimes give him bonuses. That could account for the

Mustang and my sister's boat—maybe. And the electric company *did* sometimes make mistakes.

The ghost glasses?

Maybe they were just an Eerie thing.

Right. And Hurricane Bob is just another summer afternoon thunderstorm.

There were no gangsters waiting for me at the curb. There were no gangsters anywhere downtown—or uptown, either. Still wearing my disguise, I ran down to the *Eerie Examiner* and grabbed my papers. Since my bike was back home, I had to do the route by foot. It's not a huge route, so it wasn't a big deal.

I got more nervous the closer I got to home. Even Elvis startled me. He was in the middle of his front lawn, waiting for the paper.

"Hey there, little paperboy. What's with the glasses?"

"Um, nothing."

"You ought to get some blue suede shoes to go with them."

I thanked him for the advice and went to deliver the last paper. Our house was just up the block.

It looked the way it always looked. Ordinary. Dad's Mustang was sitting in the driveway. Sun glinted off the chrome bumpers and mirror. The wild roses that grew in Mom's side garden blew in the breeze. It was all very peaceful, like a scene out of a commercial for laundry detergent.

Until I heard tires squealing around the corner. I pulled myself up and over the fence into Simon's yard and hid.

Sure enough, a purple Dream Deliveries van skidded to a stop. The back opened, and before you could say "The Godfather," a dozen guys in double-breasted suits jumped out of the door. They all carried violin cases under their arms.

Either the Eerie Symphony was giving a concert in our backyard, or the bad guys had just arrived.

I snuck along the fence toward the front of Simon's house. There were a couple of places where the slats were spread far apart and I had a good view.

These bad boys didn't believe in knocking. One of them popped open his violin case and pulled out a tommy gun. He shot a stream of bullets through our front-door lock. Then he stood back while two other gangsters banged their shoulders against the door. It looked like a scene out of *America's Most Wanted*— except the bad guys were busting in, not the cops.

They all went inside. I climbed over the fence and ran to the side of my house. Then I snuck up to the kitchen window.

It's hard to describe how hideous the scene inside was. You may want to skip the next few sentences.

Especially if you ever want to eat peanut butter and jelly again.

The first thing the gangsters did was raid the refrigerator. They found Mom's super-size grape jelly jar and her homemade peanut butter. There was enough jelly and peanut butter to make about two hundred sandwiches.

But there wasn't enough bread. In fact, there were only three slices, including the heels at the ends of the loaf.

So they used their hands. First they smeared peanut butter on their palms. Then they grabbed jelly from the jar with their fingers. A few of them were still licking away when I got to the window.

As you can imagine, there was jelly and peanut butter all over everything, including the gangsters and their guns.

Mom, Dad and Syndi cowered in the corner. They looked as scared as I've ever seen them. I guess when you see people with manners that bad, you have to fear for your life.

The messiest gangster was a big, fat fellow who wore a lime green suit. He had a cigar in his mouth. He hadn't bothered taking it out when he ate his peanut butter and jelly, so you can imagine what it looked like.

He strode to the middle of the room, leaving a trail of jam across Mom's floor. But she was too scared to complain.

"All right, youse," he said. "Lissen up. My name is Lefty Linguine, and I'm in charge."

Boy, I sure can dream them, I thought to myself. I'll bet the guy next to him was called Mario Macaroni.

He was.

"This here's Mario Macaroni. And that's Louie Lasagna."

There was an entire Italian restaurant inside. That's what I got for going to bed so hungry. From now on, I'll eat a snack or something before I go to sleep.

And maybe I'll read a dictionary or an English book or something.

"I know youse people gots connected with these dream things," said Linguine. "This here's the plan. You start dreaming big stuff now, or youse are all going to the big sleep."

"Is that a new furniture store?" my dad asked.

Linguine jabbed a sticky finger in my dad's chest. "The big sleep. One where you don't wake up. Ever."

The gangsters began herding my family upstairs to their bedrooms. As they did, one of the bad guys happened to glance out the window.

"Hey boss, there's some kid with a mustache outside. Want me to shoo him away?"

Before I could even take a step away, Linguine had spotted me. "YOU IDIOT!" he roared. "That's the kid that dreamed us. He's the one we really want. There's no telling what his imagination can invent. Grab him!"

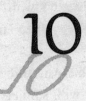

10

*L*et me give you a little advice. If you're going to dream about gangsters, don't give them very good weapons. Water pistols and slingshots are about the right speed. Even better would be feather dusters and powder puffs.

But I had given them tommy guns. A burst from one of those submachine guns could saw a piece of wood in half. So just imagine what it could do to a person.

I tried not to as I ran. In fact, I tried not to imagine anything except escape. I lost my disguise as I bolted over the fence into Simon's yard. The gangsters came right after me.

Simon hadn't finished counting all the toy soldiers he'd been playing with the day before. They were still piled up around the yard. I ran right through them. The gangsters followed. With all the jelly they had slobbered on themselves, they were stickier than a bad report card. The toys stuck to their feet and legs as they ran, slowing them down. The little guys with the bayonets were the worst. The gangsters yelped in pain as they ran through them.

Before they were halfway through Simon's army, the crooks were covered with soldiers. Still, they kept coming. Plastic soldiers aren't a match for imaginary gangsters.

But that did give me an idea. I bolted down the block, running toward B.F. Skinner Junior High. By now, one of the gangsters had found the keys to Dad's Mustang. A whole bunch of them piled in. They roared down the block after me. I ducked down Thirteenth Avenue, running toward Edgar Allan Poe Boulevard.

They almost caught up to me when I reached O'Brien's Real Italian Delicatessen on Pigout Lane. I ducked inside. There was an alley behind the store that led directly to the junior high. I hoped I could get there and regain my lead.

But the gangsters were too quick. They roared around the back before I could get out. I skidded to a stop at the back door, wondering what to do.

Sometimes, even in Eerie, luck takes over. Mrs. O'Brien had made a fresh batch of garlic salami the night before. It was hanging in the back room, drying out. As soon as the gangsters got out of the car to look for me, they smelled it. Hungry as ever, they pushed through the back door and started grabbing for it.

That gave me just the chance I needed. I turned around and zipped out the front door and down the street quicker than a cat in a dog pound.

B.F. Skinner lay dead ahead. I ran across the front lawn for all I was worth. Behind me, one of the gangsters shouted to the others to get back in the car.

The only thing worse than being chased by mobsters with submachine guns is being chased by mobsters with submachine guns and garlic salami on their breath. If the wind had shifted in my direction I would have suffocated.

Because of summer vacation, the front door of the school was locked. But one of the nearby classroom windows was wide open. And as luck would have it, it was Mr. Biosphere's room—exactly where I wanted to go.

It didn't take long for my gangster buddies to catch up. Two of them stayed outside to guard against my escape. The others broke down the front door and started looking for me. I heard a janitor scream. Then the door to the classroom burst open, and a half-dozen gangsters with really bad breath entered the room.

I edged backwards against the display case. An entire semester's worth of science projects sat behind me.

There were exploding volcanoes, electromagnetic nails, a frog that could croak the theme song from the *Brady Bunch*.

And Simon's giant ant farm.

"Okay, kid, the jig is up. You're coming back to the house with us," said Mario Macaroni. One of Simon's toy soldiers was pasted to his cheek. "You have some serious dreaming to do."

"Let's see you make me."

"With pleasure," said Macaroni. "Get him, boys."

With that, the rest of the gang charged.

I turned and yanked open the display panel. With all my might, I grabbed Simon's science project and threw it to the ground.

Those giant ants had been cooped up in the glass case for so long they were dying to get some real exercise. They were also hungry as anything—all Mr. Biosphere had given them to eat was healthy stuff like oranges and apple bits. The jelly clinging to the gangsters was the first good gooey meal they'd smelled in days. As soon as the glass shattered, those ants made an "ant line" toward them.

They gnawed at their pants and suits like piranhas dismantling a cow. The gangsters tried swatting them away, but Eerie ants are tougher than your average ant. The bad guys forgot about me and tried to run for it.

Most dove through the window onto the front lawn. But the ants kept right after them, gnawing and slurping in every direction.

I didn't have much time to gloat. There were still a half-dozen gangsters back at my house. That included the ringleader, Lefty Linguine. I knew from my nightmare that Linguine was in a class by himself. If they put his poster up on the wall in the post office all of the other wanted posters would run away in fright.

How do you get rid of a dream come true? I have to admit I had no idea. In fact, I really didn't know that much about dreams at all.

I decided I had better study up. I headed over to the Eerie Library to do some quick research.

The librarian looked at me kind of funny when I asked.

"Books on stopping dreams?" Mrs. Piddlefeather wrinkled her nose. For a second I wondered if the gangsters' garlic breath was still clinging to my clothes. "Are you having nightmares?"

"Something like that."

She got up from her desk and led me up the stairs to the second floor, where all the nonfiction books were kept. We walked past a shelf full of bird books. The chirping was so loud it was hard to hear myself think.

The books on dreams were kept in the Head Stuff room. A plaque on the door said the collection inside was dedicated to Dr. Harvey Wallbanger, Eerie's first psychologist. He was also a big game hunter. Besides the books, the room was filled with shrunken heads. The display didn't explain whether he had found the heads on his hunting trips, or if they had been his patients.

Mrs. Piddlefeather saw me staring at the heads and cleared her throat. "Are you interested in dreams, or skulls?"

"Dreams," I said, dragging myself from the display.

"This might be what you're looking for." The librarian pulled a volume from the shelves. *"Controlling Your Nightmare."*

I took the book from her and sat at a nearby table to look at it. Written by man named I. Ken Snore, it was about three inches thick, with really small type. That was impressive, but I didn't get too far before realizing it wasn't the book for me.

Snore said the best way to deal with a nightmare was to face it directly. "Spit in its eye and laugh," he said.

That wouldn't work with Lefty Linguine.

I went back to the shelf and looked at the other books there. Most were about what dreams meant. For example, did you ever have a dream about going to school in your underwear? If so, did you know that your dream is really about the fact that there are more fish in the ocean than you can eat in one day?

At least that's what one book said. It was like a dictionary of dreams. Nothing really meant what it seemed to when you dreamed it. Dreaming is a little like being in Eerie, I guess.

The dream dictionary didn't give me any ideas on how to get rid of the gangsters. But the book next to it did. It was by Dr. Horace Somalax, and it was called *Positive Sleep.*

According to Dr. Somalax, a person can actually plan his dream before he goes to bed. In fact, Dr. Somalax said, that was the key to living a good life. "Dream well, live well is my motto," he declared.

I don't know about that, but it did give me a plan. If I could dream up the gangsters, I could dream up someone to get rid of them. The biggest enemies gangsters had during Prohibition were G-men. Mr. Radford had told us all about them. So all I had to do was dream up some G-men and Linguine's mob would be yesterday's lunch.

"Read a book before you go to bed," Dr. Somalax suggested in his book. "It will help you relax. Even better—it will direct your dreams."

So I checked out every book the library had on the FBI. Then I went to find a good place to take a nap.

11

The best place in Eerie to take a nap is in the back row of Ms. Demerol's class. Since school was out for the summer, that was no good.

A lot of places tie for second, including the bed display in World of Stuff. That's such a good place I found Mr. Radford using it when I went there after the library. He was curled around the pillow and looked so peaceful I just couldn't disturb him. So instead I took off my shoes and curled up in a corner of the biggest sofa in his furniture section.

I started reading one of the books, *Mr. FBI: J. Edgar Hoover*. J. Edgar Hoover was the head of the Federal Bureau of Investigation for about a million years, starting during Prohibition. The book wasn't really boring enough to put me to sleep, so I searched through my pile for another. A really thin book called *The FBI and Animal Rights* looked promising. Then I found one with really small type called *FBI Protocol and Procedure*

Manual, Conveyed in Citizens' Terminology. Since I couldn't even understand the title, I knew this was the book for me. Sure enough, I got through only a few sentences before my eyelids started to feel heavy.

But I dozed off for only a few minutes. I didn't really have enough time to get a good dream in. All my sleeping mind could conjure was a picture of those shrunken heads at the library. That and a big blue swordfish flopping around in Ms. Demerol's health class, wearing someone's underwear.

I decided to try again. I should have been really tired. After all, I had spent the night sitting between a big scale and a fortune teller booth. This time I looked for a book that I could understand. I hoped it would give my dreams a head start. The one I found was about how the FBI captured John Dillinger. It had pictures and everything. Unfortunately the book was pretty exciting. In fact, it was so exciting that it left me wide awake. Forget about catching forty winks. I couldn't even grab a half wink.

After about an hour's worth of reading, I tried to close my eyes and force myself to dream. But that didn't work. A couple of members of Eerie's only motorcycle gang came into World of Stuff and started making a ruckus.

In the rest of the universe, motorcycle gangs have

names like *Hell's Angels,* and they go around drinking beer and starting fights. In Eerie, they call themselves The Unkind Oncs, and they drink stuff like orange soda and ginger ale. They tell bad jokes, and make funny faces at people. Then they help you find lost stuff, or carry your groceries home.

They don't tangle with gangsters, though.

"Not our rap," said the gang leader when I asked.

Out of ideas and unable to get to sleep, I decided to sneak back over to my house. I wanted to find out if the gangsters were still there. Also, I thought I might be able to get Simon to help.

On the way over, I tried daydreaming a little. Daydreaming is a poor substitute for sleep, but I figured, why not? I daydreamed about FBI agents, J. Edgar Hoover, and a whole room filled with hairy-legged ballerinas.

I don't know where that last idea came from. It didn't matter though. There were no ballerinas or G-men on the block that I could see. And if J. Edgar Hoover had come by, he must have gone inside to have tea with Elvis.

The gangsters were still around, though. I spied on my house from behind a tree three yards away. One of the thugs was sitting right in the middle of the driveway. He had pulled out the easy chair from the living room.

He'd also set up some soda cans at the edge of the curb for target practice. He leaned back in the recliner and fired a spray of bullets from his tommy gun.

He hit about half of the cans. Those weren't great odds, especially if you were bigger than a soda can.

I was just trying to figure out how I could get to Simon's house without him spotting me when I heard a van approaching. Sure enough, Dream Deliveries was making another run.

Had my daydreaming worked? I peered around the side of the tree trunk. The deliveryman jumped out of the truck and grabbed a package from the back. It was long, but not big enough to have a squad of FBI agents in it.

Whatever was inside did seem to be alive, though. The box practically jumped out of his arms.

The gangster went to help him. "Whatcha got?"

"They never tell me," said the deliveryman. "They just give me a box and an address."

"Must be a boring job."

"Nah. Deliveries are my life."

Just then the box squirted out of his hands. It was easy to see what it was now. A long, sharp sword slashed through the brown cardboard as the rest of the package thrashed in the grass.

The swordfish I'd dreamed before.

"Tell you what. I have another package," the deliveryman told the gangster. "You bring this inside and I'll get the other one."

The package was huge—so big the deliveryman had to use a cart to get it out and up to the front door.

This one was big enough to hold G-men. Or at least J. Edgar Hoover and a ballerina.

I was sorely tempted to sneak up to the window and watch as it was opened inside. But I realized I had something more important to do. Here was a chance to meet the Dream Delivery people in person. I could stow away in the back of the truck. Sooner or later, the driver would have to head back to his warehouse. There, I could talk to whoever was in charge and stop the dream deliveries.

After I had a special order of G-men sent to clean up Linguine and the rest of the fruits and vegetables inside.

As soon as the deliveryman had his package inside the front door, I bolted for the van. Just as I grabbed the handle, the door flew open. I spun to the pavement, thrown down by a whirling tornado.

12

"Out of my way!" the tornado screamed as I rolled on the ground. "LEFTY LINGUINE, JUNIOR, I KNOW YOU'RE IN THERE! COME OUT THIS MINUTE!"

It took a few seconds before I realized it wasn't a tornado at all. I had been knocked down by an old lady dressed completely in black. She wore a heavy veil. A patent leather pocketbook the size of Rhode Island swung from her arm.

Lefty Linguine and his lime green suit appeared on the front step. He had the box that had just been delivered in his hand.

"Who dreamed up these shrunken heads?" he demanded, holding one up.

"There you are!" yelled the old lady.

Linguine took one look and started back inside. "Aw, Ma, what are you doing here?"

"What am I doing here? What are you doing including me in your nightmares, young man?'' Mrs. Linguine grabbed him by the ear and started dragging him off down the block.

"You're going to get the whipping of your life," his mother told him. "You and your friends have been running around shooting up the neighborhood again, haven't you?"

"But all the gangsters do it."

"Name one."

"Al Capone."

"Al Capone! Al Capone! That's all I ever hear. Al Capone this, Al Capone that. Wait until I call his mother. I don't think *she* lets him drive around with a tommy gun."

"But Ma-aa!"

Just then a broken-down wreck of a car squealed around the corner and headed for my driveway. It was my dad's dream Mustang. All the paint had been stripped off. The tires were flat and the doors caved in. The horse that had been on the grill was now a bare skeleton. The ants had worked that car over good.

They'd also done a number on the gangsters. Their clothes were in tatters. Red welts covered their faces and arms where the ants had bitten them.

Needless to say, they weren't in a good mood. But

then how would you feel if a giant ant farm treated you like a Happy Meal?

"There's that bratty kid!" Macaroni exclaimed. The tire rims threw up sparks as the driver veered in my direction. "Let's get him!"

Talk about your recurring nightmares. I scrambled across the lawn as the gangsters drove the wheezing Mustang up on the grass after me. Faking left, I ran to the right. When I reached the fence to Simon's yard, I threw my hands to the top and vaulted with all my might.

"*Psst*—Marshall! Here! Quick!"

Simon was peering out from beneath the old-fashioned steel door to his basement. The door covered the stairwell. I scrambled to it as he held it open. As soon I was on the steps, he closed it as quietly as he could.

Neither one of us spoke for at least a minute. We could hear the gangsters running around to the gate. They began searching the yard. Our hearts practically stopped beating when one of them plopped down on top of the door.

Luckily for me I hadn't dreamed very smart gangsters. They were not very organized, and were definitely bad at hide-and-seek. They wandered around Simon's backyard, looking in only the most obvious places.

Finally we heard Macaroni shout to the others. He

said he was in charge, now that Linguine had left. Grumbling, he told the others to quit running around. He wanted them back inside my house where they could get changed.

We waited silently to make sure the mobsters weren't just trying to trick us. Then I told Simon what had happened. He was a little sad that his ants had escaped. But he figured it was for a good cause.

"Besides," he said, "this means I won't have to go back to school until September."

"We may never go back to school if we can't get rid of the rest of these gangsters," I told him, explaining my plan. "You have to help me dream up some FBI agents."

"Sometimes, if I'm watching a horror movie on TV, I dream about it later," said Simon. "Maybe that would work now. If there was a movie about cops or something."

He led the way through his basement. A small TV-room was set up on the other side of the furnace room. We flipped through the channels for a while, looking for a police show. All we could find were talk shows and soap operas. The closest thing to drama we could find was *Tell Eerie, Girlfriend*. It was a talk show. Three ladies sat around a table and yakked about how terrible it was to break a fingernail on your way to a UFO sighting.

Simon flipped through the channels three times before giving up. He tuned into the station that had been playing the *Lassie/Lost In Space* marathon the other day. Now they were showing Abbott & Costello movies, nonstop.

"This is a great movie," said Simon, putting down the remote control. *"Abbott and Costello Meet Frankenstein."*

I don't know whether it was the movie or what, but suddenly a great idea flew into my head. I jumped up with a shout.

"I didn't know you were that big an Abbott and Costello fan," said Simon.

"No, I just figured out how to get rid of the gangsters."

"Cut off cable to your house?"

"No. What's worse than a nightmare?"

"A math exam that you haven't studied for?"

"Well, yeah, that too. But what I was thinking was, a *real* nightmare. What if our gangster friends met up with the ghosts in haunted house number twenty-six? We get the gangsters over there with the ghost glasses, and the ghosts will take care of the rest. They hate being seen."

"How are you going to get them to wear the glasses?" asked Simon. "And how are you going to get them to go over to the house?"

I didn't have the slightest idea yet. But you know what they say: Necessity is the mother of invention.

Except in Eerie. Here weirdness is the mother of invention. Necessity is more like a second cousin. But I knew Simon and I could think of *something*.

13

"*E*XTRA, EXTRA, READ ALL ABOUT IT! LOCAL KID DISCOVERS ENTRANCE TO DREAM GOLD MINE. EERIE RESIDENT NOW A DREAM-COME-TRUE MILLIONAIRE. EXTRA, EXTRA! READ ALLLLLLL ABOUT IT!''

The front door to my house flew open. Just as Simon and I had suspected, the gangsters were way too greedy to pass up bait like that. Macaroni himself came out of the house and grabbed the newspaper from Simon's hand.

If you looked at it closely, you would realize that it wasn't a real copy of the *Eerie Examiner.* For one thing, the *Examiner* would never misspell its own name on the front page. But the dreamed-up crooks were too stupid to know that, as Simon had pointed out after we printed up the copy.

The real *Examiner* was also twice as big as the piece of paper Simon's dad's computer had printed out. But the story could have been on toilet paper for all Macaroni cared. He only wanted to know what it said.

"Read it to me," he told Simon. "And go slow, so I understand."

Simon took the paper back and began to read the story he and I had composed. "Local kid Marshall Teller today discovered the secret entrance to an abandoned Eerie gold mine. The gold mine contains at least one million dollars in nuggets, according to reliable sources. Marshall Teller told this reporter that finding the gold mine was a dream come true."

"That rotten brat has been holding out on us," said Macaroni. "Where is this mine?"

Simon continued to read. "The location of the mine remains a closely guarded secret. However, Marshall Teller was last seen near the Gambino casino on the north end of town—"

Macaroni pushed Simon to the ground and ran inside the house.

"Wait!" shouted Simon. "You didn't hear the rest of the story. To find the mine shaft, you have to wear special glasses! Wait! Wait!"

Simon had brought the box of ghost glasses that he took home with him earlier to the front door. We had pasted a new cover on it: SECRET GOLD MINE GLASSES

INSIDE. The gangsters were supposed to read that, then grab the glasses.

They were in too much of a hurry. Before Simon could do anything else, they ran out of the house to the battered Mustang. They jumped into, onto and under the car, holding on as it squealed out of the driveway. Shooting sparks in all directions, they careened toward the Gambino casino at full speed.

Meanwhile, I was waiting at the haunted house. I kept my ghost glasses in my pocket. The ghosts had already made it very clear that they didn't like to be looked at.

Everything looked exactly as Simon and I had left it the other day. Our footprints were still visible in the dust. Without the glasses, even the gambling room looked quiet.

I'm pretty bad at waiting around doing nothing. There's only so many times you can recite the alphabet backwards to yourself, or sing "One Hundred Bottles of Beer on the Wall." Sooner or later, you start feeling antsy.

I decided to go up on the balcony and wait. After a while I checked the door marked NAUGHTY NANNIES. It was still locked. I sat near the railing, telling myself over and over that I had to be patient.

I took the ghost glasses out of my pocket and inspected them. They seemed like ordinary glasses in every way. Even the lenses looked like the kind you use to see regular stuff.

Now you are probably thinking that having the glasses in my hand was too much temptation. If you had ghost glasses and were sitting in a room full of ghosts, you would probably put them on. And you think I'm just like you.

You're right.

Even though I knew it was dangerous, I decided to take a tiny peek. After all, it would make sense to see where most of the ghosts were, right? And who knew when I might get a chance to look again?

My hands were trembling a little as I tilted them in front of my eyes. I planned to whisk them away after a quick glance. No use taking unnecessary chances.

But I couldn't believe what I saw.

Nothing.

Not one ghost gambling at the card tables. Not one pale woman standing near the bar asking for a drink. Not one shadowy man in an old-fashioned suit checking his pocket for cash. There was no one around the roulette table, no one in the cashier's box, nobody guarding the door.

The place was empty.

I took the glasses off and blinked my eyes. Then I

jammed the glasses back on. Nothing. I took them off and wiped the lenses on my shirt. Nothing. I blinked, I nodded, I perspired. Nothing, nothing, nothing.

"Hey! There he is!"

The voice sounded horrible and ghoulish. It filled me with joy—the place was still haunted after all. I turned to get a good look at the ghosts.

Which is when I realized they weren't ghosts at all. They were the gangsters, piling out of the door marked NAUGHTY NANNIES. They must have come in through a back entrance or something.

"Grab him, boys!" shouted Macaroni.

I took a step toward the stairs before I realized two goons were climbing up them. Desperate, I swung over the side of the railing. I hung down, then let go.

The table I landed on crashed to the floor beneath me. As I stumbled to get up, one of the gangster creeps aimed his tommy gun at me. Somehow I managed to dive out of the way as a stream of bullets exploded over my head.

"You idiot!" screamed Macaroni. "Don't shoot him! We need him alive so we can find out where this gold mine is. Then we kill him."

Two of the gangsters jumped from the balcony to the bar at the other end of the room. They were between me and the hole in the wall near the fake library. Another appeared in front of the hole to the outside hallway.

But I wasn't taking either exit. I ran to the roulette wheel as Macaroni clambered down the stairs, huffing and puffing.

"Hey Mario, you feeling lucky?" I yelled. Then I pushed the button to open the trap door.

Falling feet first through the hatch, I began thinking of a new plan to outwit these dim bulbs. One good dream and they'd be history. Maybe I'd go over to the church for a service—people were always falling asleep during the sermons. Or maybe I could look up Ms. Demerol and ask to enroll in summer school.

I tucked my feet under my body as I fell. I closed my eyes. I hadn't hit my head this time, so I knew it would be okay. It was a short fall. I knew what to expect.

Which is why I almost had a heart attack when my feet didn't bounce off the mattress. In fact, they didn't bounce at all.

I had jumped right into the outstretched arms of a gangster.

"I'm feeling real lucky today," said Macaroni from above. "How about you?"

I guess they thought tying me facedown to the roulette wheel was fun, because they laughed and giggled while they did it. And they must have thought giving it a spin was even funnier, because they roared out loud every time Macaroni sent me revolving.

"Hey boss, put a ball in his mouth. Let's see what number comes up."

"Shut up, you fools," said Macaroni. "This is serious business." He stopped me from spinning. "You, kid. You found this gold mine, right? Where is it?"

"Gold mine? What gold mine?"

"Don't give me that. I know you found a gold mine."

"There's no gold mine here," I said.

He gave the wheel another spin. My head felt like it was going to shoot off to Mars. I've listened to lectures from my dad, but they didn't send my head spinning *this* fast.

"You going to tell me what I want to know?" Macaroni asked when the wheel stopped.

"If you spin me again, I'll lose my breakfast."

"Sounds like a personal hygiene problem to me," said Macaroni. Even so, he took his hand off the wheel. "Where's the opening to the mine shaft?"

"You need special glasses to see it," I said.

"Special glasses? What kind of bull is that?"

"It's the truth. You need special glasses. I lost mine in the house somewhere when you were chasing me.

Honest. You can't see the mine shaft without the glasses."

"Sounds like a fairy tale to me," said Macaroni. "And I don't like fairy tales."

"Hey boss, look at these," said one of the goons. "I found a pair of crushed eyeglasses on the floor."

Macaroni took the glasses. The lens were totally broken and mangled.

"There's nothing special about these glasses," he said. "Here, Sonny—get me one of those bowling balls from the car. Let's see how our little friend here likes gambling."

"SECRET MINE SHAFT GLASSES, TEN CENTS APIECE! GET YOUR MINE SHAFT GLASSES! ONLY A DIME! GET 'EM WHILE THEY'RE HOT!"

Good ol' Simon. Always showing up in the nick of time. I couldn't see him. I couldn't see anything but the number 13 because I was tied to the roulette wheel face down. But I knew he must have come up with a plan to rescue me.

The only problem was that the ghosts were gone. I knew I had to warn him. Once they realized the glasses wouldn't lead them to any gold, the gangsters were going to be plenty angry.

"Get out of here, Simon! Run! Split! Adios! *Hasta la vista!* Take the last train to Clarksville!"

"Shut up, kid," said Macaroni. He took the wheel and gave it a spin so hard I thought I was going to screw down right through the table.

"All right, grab the little kid with the glasses and let's check this story out. This better be on the level," I heard Macaroni tell Simon. "If it ain't, you'll be sharing some cement slippers with your buddy here."

Then they led him off into another part of the house.

14

I spun around that wheel for a long time. But the wait after it stopped was even longer.

Maybe that's because I knew I was waiting for the final countdown, the big sleep, the last resort. With no ghosts to scare these goons off, I was a goner.

Even worse, Simon was a goner, too. That might have been the absolute worst thing. If it hadn't been for me, Simon would never have come here. He wouldn't have tangled with the gangsters at all. Heck, he never even would have seen how weird Eerie was. If I had never moved here from New Jersey, he would have gone through life thinking weird was normal.

Even with all the weirdness, I never expected to go out like this. Strapped to a gambling wheel, one big, human, unlucky number.

The number 13, to be exact. Right under my nose.

I stared at that number a long time. When I finally heard the footsteps coming for me in the distance, it was almost a relief. They were very far off, and they walked very slowly. Still, I knew they were coming for me. And I guess I was ready to meet my maker.

Or at least the cement mixer.

I could hear somebody calling my name. I didn't answer. I wasn't going to give them the satisfaction of begging for my life. I was going out with my head held high, a Teller through and through.

Actually, my head was held low, because I was tied down.

I closed my eyes, waiting.

When something touched my back, it felt a lot lighter than I expected. It was more like a tap than a slap. It might even have felt friendly.

Another trick to get me to lower my guard. I wasn't falling for it.

My knots were untied. They were going to carry me off to my doom.

But not without a fight!

I spun around, flailing my arms. I managed to get one blow in. My attacker fell to the ground.

"Hey, what gives?" he yelped.

It was Simon.

"Simon. How'd you get away?"

"All the gangsters took off as soon as I read that

newspaper story to them," he said, rubbing his chest where I hit him.

"The story? Here?"

"No. Back at the house. They jumped in the Mustang and drove over here. Why didn't you answer when I called you? Or when I slapped you on your back?"

"Simon, that wasn't you who gave them the ghost glasses?"

"The ghost glasses are right here," he said, pointing to the box on the floor. "They wouldn't take them."

15

*S*imon and I looked at each other for a second. Then we dove for the glasses.

But when we put them on, we were just as baffled. The room was empty. No ghosts, no gangsters.

"Macaroni's goons lassoed me downstairs," I told Simon. "Maybe that's where they are now."

We went to the trapdoor overlooking the jail room and peered down. But there was nothing inside that we could see. Then we heard the sound of a brass band coming from somewhere upstairs.

The Naughty Nannies.

I wasn't sure what to do at first. I remembered how Mr. Radford had blinked his eyes and blushed. Simon was just a little kid. He wasn't ready for blushing kind of stuff.

Still, I had to see what was happening to the gangsters. There was no way I could leave Simon behind. It might not be safe.

"I may have to cover your eyes," I warned him. We went up the balcony steps and walked along the railing toward the "Naughty Nannies" door.

The door was slightly ajar. Music was definitely coming from inside. There was laughing and cheering.

I pushed open the door. It took a second for our eyes to adjust to the light. When they did, we realized that we were standing at the back of another balcony. But this one was huge. It had rows and rows of seats on it.

It was an old-fashioned theater with an upstairs section, which is where we were standing. It was super fancy, with a thick rug under our feet and sleek paneling along the side. The rows in front of us were filled with ghosts. They were all dressed in clothes from the 1920s. And they were all watching the stage.

They didn't notice Simon and me as we walked down toward the front to get a better view. They laughed and cheered at whatever was going on. In fact, they practically drowned out the band.

So what was this show they were all *haw-hawing* about?

Five grandma ghosts dressed in Little Bo-Peep costumes were doing a dance on the stage. Every so often they swayed back and did a curtsy.

The ghosts roared.

"Are those the Naughty Nannies?" Simon asked.

I shrugged. We had to elbow next to two ghosts at the edge of the rail to get a better view. They didn't seem to mind. Downstairs, the rest of the theater was packed. There must have been two or three hundred ghosts here.

If only I had brought my camera!

The grandma ghosts suddenly jumped up in the air and came down in a split. Even though you expect ghosts to be able to do that kind of thing, it was pretty cool. The audience gave them a standing ovation and they left the stage.

"What happened to Macaroni and the mobsters?" Simon asked.

Before I could shush him, a ghost turned to him.

"They're next," he said cheerfully.

And so they were. When the grandmas cleared the stage, a man dressed in a white tuxedo came out. I recognized the handlebar mustache immediately. It was the same ghost who had thrown us into the pond the first day we tried the ghost glasses.

"LAY-DEEZ AND GHOULS, LAY-DEEZ AND GHOULS," he shouted.

Everybody in the auditorium started laughing harder. It must have been some sort of joke that only ghosts get.

"But seriously folks," he said. "Now it's time for our main attraction, the Naughty Nannies!"

The band started up, but it was hard to hear the music with all the clapping. I inched my hands close to Simon's eyes as the curtain flew open.

It revealed twelve ghostly billy goats—or maybe I should say nanny goats. They were dressed in striped bathing suits and black derby hats.

They weren't alone, though. Macaroni and the rest of the gang were onstage with them. Tied up and gagged. One by one, the gangsters were head-butted into the air. The goats took turns juggling them back and forth. Before long, all twelve mobsters were flying above the stage. They were human juggling pins for the Naughty Nannies show.

The goats widened their circle. The gangsters started flying all around the auditorium. Meanwhile, some ghostly stagehands wheeled twelve large tubs of tar into the middle of the stage. Two big hay wagons with feathers were then placed on either end. The music changed, and there was a drum roll. When the drum stopped, the nannies flipped over onto their backs and shot the gangsters straight up. Each one landed with a plop in his own special tar bath. Rebounding, the gangsters flew into the feathers. Macaroni and the boys hightailed it off stage and out of our lives as quickly as they could, wearing more feathers than the average crow.

EPILOGUE

*S*imon and I didn't hang around to catch the next act. As far as we were concerned, there was no way to top the one we'd just seen. Besides, if there's one thing I've learned in Eerie, it's quit while you're ahead.

When we got back to the house, we discovered that Mom, Dad, and Syndi were fine. In fact, they didn't understand why I was so excited to see them.

"B—but the gangsters—" I stuttered.

"Oh, they weren't much of a bother," said my mom. "Except for their table manners, I hardly noticed they were here."

"But they tied you up!"

"Gave me a chance to meditate," said my dad. "I haven't been able to clear my mind for months."

That's my family for you—they always make the best of everything.

"One of them helped me study for my driver's test,"

said Syndi. "Did you know that if you go to pass some-one and they won't move over, it's okay to shoot out their tires?"

I told my sister she had better check the manual on that one.

Simon and I decided we needed to celebrate our adventures with some Black Cows at World of Stuff. We knew if we hung around much longer, Mom would put us to work scraping jelly and peanut butter off the floor.

"How goes the ghost hunting?" Mr. Radford asked as soon as we walked into the shop.

"It's been a dream," I said sarcastically. That's when I realized we were still just one nightmare away from real disaster. I excused myself and went over to the phone booth to try calling Dream Deliveries one more time.

To my total amazement, the phone rang.

And rang, and rang, and rang.

I was just about to hang up when someone finally answered.

"Hello?" said the sleepy voice.

"Hello, is this Dream Deliveries?"

"Yes."

"This is Marshall Teller. You've been making deliveries to my house and—"

"Service has been suspended to the Teller residence for lack of payment," snapped the lady. "If you wish to resume service—"

I hung up before she could finish.

Over at the counter, Mr. Radford was just plopping our drinks down.

"Sounds like you had quite a bit of fun over at the old Gambino casino." He winked as I slid onto a seat. "Those Naughty Nannies are something, aren't they?"

"You've seen them?"

Mr. Radford only winked and blushed. "The curtseying grandmothers are a bit racy for my taste, but all in all, it's quite a show."

"Pure Eerie," I said, sipping my Black Cow.

We were having a typical Sunday afternoon at my house. I remember the day very clearly, because Sunday is Swedish Cutlet Day. Swedish Cutlets are my dad's favorite food. He likes them better than deep-dish pepperoni pizza with extra sauce and cheese. Me, I like them okay, but not any better than, say, rice and bloody cow brains.

Just kidding. I don't like rice at all.

Mom had just gotten back from giving Syndi driving lessons. Fortunately they only practiced in the school parking lot or they might never have gotten back at all. But let me stick to one scary story at a time.

Dad was sitting at the kitchen table putting together the latest model in the *Giants of the Bottom of the Sea* series, the HMS *Titanic*. I was munching on some popcorn and reading an article in the Sunday *Eerie Examiner* titled "Corn. The Untold Story."

One second, everything was peaceful. The next second, Mom was backing away from the open refrigerator, shrieking.

"There's something bleeding in there!" she screamed. "It's alive!"

"It's just my science project, Mom," I said. "What's the big deal?"

"Marshall, look at this thing," she said, pulling the door open wide.

Blood splurted out from the center shelf. Even I gulped for a second.

Our class was studying something called capillary action. It's a way for water to defy gravity. It means that if you put a piece of celery in a glass of water, the water will rise up through the celery. If you use red food dye, then you can see how this works: the veins in the celery become red.

Using celery would have been boring, so I decided to use cauliflower. Better than eating it, right? According to our textbook, the white top of the cauliflower should have turned red. But something weird was going on with my science project. The capillary action was working too well. That cauliflower was spurting tinted water out of its top stronger than Old Faithful.

Only in Eerie. Apparently gravity is a lot easier to defy here than in the rest of the world, something I should have figured.

"You better clean up that refrigerator, young man," said my mom. "Look—the cutlets are ruined. There goes dinner."

The cutlets had been sitting right under my experiment. There was so much food dye in the plate they looked like beets.

"It's only food dye," I explained, getting a sponge.

"They're drenched with water. They'll taste horrible, not to mention how they look. Now we have nothing for dinner."

"You have more in the freezer," said my dad, trying to be helpful.

"Those are frozen," Mom said.

"That's okay." Dad finished gluing the anchor on his model and got up. "The Gorillamatic Techna Rotta Griller will defrost them in a jiff. In fact, it'll whip up the whole dinner in five minutes flat."

Mom made a face. "Edgar, honey, I don't know about using that thing to cook dinner."

"It's the latest in high-tech cooking," said my dad, patting the machine. He had set it up on the counter that morning. "Relax, hon. We'll be enjoying Swedish cutlets in no time."

"It ruined breakfast," said Mom.

"No, it didn't. I like my eggs well done."

"But not with the shells in them."

"That was my mistake. I forgot to turn the calcium setting off. Besides, now I won't have to drink milk for a week."

My father works for Things, Inc. He tests all sorts of new stuff to see if it works. The idea is that if it works here in Eerie, it will work anywhere. Statistically speaking, Eerie is the most normal place in the world.

You know what they say about statistics, right? In my experience, if it works in Eerie, it has a good chance of not working anywhere else. This is the center of weirdness for the entire universe—the Bermuda Triangle of reality.

The Gorillamatic Techna Rotta Griller looked like a copy machine, except that there was a stack of dishes where the paper would go. You put your food on top, fiddled with the settings, and then things started humming. Dinner popped out on each plate, ready to eat.

At least that's what the instruction manual said.

"This will be the perfect test," said my father. "You're not jealous, are you?"

"Jealous? Of a cooking machine?" said my mom.

Dad put his arms around Mom and got a kind of goofy look in his eyes. "You're worried that if a machine can cook, what will you do, right? You're worried that I won't love you anymore."

"But Edgar—"

"I'll always love you, Marilyn. You can count on that. Machines are just tools. They give us more time to do the things we love, like taking Syndi for driving lessons."

"We should get a machine for that."

Instead of answering, Dad kissed her. They do that lovey-dovey stuff all the time. It's part of the downside of being married, I guess.

Mom finally agreed to use the Rotta Griller. "But if it ruins the cutlets," she warned, "you're taking us out to eat."

"It won't ruin the cutlets," said my dad. "I promise."

If I had any doubts about how this would turn out, they vanished right then. Because on just about the first day I came to Eerie I learned never to make a promise about anything you can't control. If you do, it will blow up in your face.

Which is what the Gorilla Techna Rotta Griller did about two minutes after Mom started it up.

"Incoming! Hit the deck!" she screamed as the machine began spitting dishes and cutlets around the kitchen. Bread crumbs and cream of tomato soup shot all over the place. After thirty seconds of sheer terror, the kitchen looked like a meatloaf turned inside out.

Fortunately the only casualty besides dinner was my dad's model. He had just arranged the deck chairs when the bow shot up and then nosed straight to the floor. The *Titanic* had been sunk by a slab of veal.

Syndi, Mom, and I started cleaning up. "Here's the problem!" Dad said, inspecting the Rotta Griller. "The popcorn setting was on. Now who used the machine to make popcorn?"

I pretended I didn't hear the question.

THINGS CAN'T GET ANY EERIER
...OR CAN THEY?

Don't miss a single book!

#1: Return to Foreverware
by Mike Ford
79774-7/$.99 US/$.99 Can

#2: Bureau of Lost
by John Peel
79775-5/$3.99 US/$4.99 Can

#3: The Eerie Triangle
by Mike Ford
79776-3/$3.99 US/$4.99 Can

#4: Simon and Marshall's Excellent Adventure
by John Peel
79777-1/$3.99 US/$4.99 Can

#5: Have Yourself an Eerie Little Christmas
by Mike Ford
79781-X/$3.99 US/$4.99 Can

#6: Fountain of Weird
by Sherry Shahan
79782-8/$3.99 US/$4.99 Can

#7: Attack of the Two-Ton Tomatoes
by Mike Ford
79783-6/$3.99 US/$4.99 Can

#8: Who Framed Alice Prophet?
by Mike Ford
79784-4/$3.99 US/$4.99 Can